The Revenge of Samuel Stokes

The figure on the television screen began to fade. Its voice became more distant. "See to it! I will have no dealings with the peasantry. Be warned of what I may do!"

The table rocked slowly to and fro, overturning Grandpa's cup. The sofa rolled forward by several inches. The carpet, quite distinctly, rippled. Outside, blackbirds rushed about the garden shrieking.

When things returned to normal, two seconds later, there was a crack down the plaster of one wall and a fine network of lines on the ceiling. "That does it!" said Mrs Thornton grimly. "Subsidence or no subsidence, we're not going on like this. There'll have to be an emergency meeting."

Grandpa and the children were silent. They looked at the cracks, at the spilled tea, and at each other.

ALSO BY PENELOPE LIVELY

Astercote
The Driftway
Fanny and the Monsters
The Ghost of Thomas Kempe
Going Back
The House in Norham Gardens
A Stitch in Time
The Voyage of QV66
The Whispering Knights
The Wild Hunt of Hagworthy

The Revenge of Samuel Stokes

by PENELOPE LIVELY

MAMMOTH

First published in Great Britain 1981
by William Heinemann Ltd
Published 1991 by Mammoth
an imprint of Reed Consumer Books Limited
Michelin House, 81 Fulham Road, London SW3 6RB
and Auckland, Melbourne, Singapore and Toronto

Reprinted 1991 (twice), 1992, 1993

ISBN 0 7497 0601 5

A CIP catalogue record for this title
is available from the British Library

Printed and bound in Great Britain
by Cox & Wyman Ltd, Reading, Berkshire

to Betty and to Jane

CHAPTER I

You may well ask how a smell of roast venison could come out of Mrs Thornton's washing-machine, or tobacco smoke from a television set, or how a housing estate could be flooded by a lake that did not exist. You may, like Great Maxton District Council, insist that there is some perfectly simple and ordinary explanation, if only someone could lay their hands on it. You may, like the newspapers, consider that the inhabitants of Charstock were a nutty lot anyway, and exaggerated the whole thing. There is a professor from a university who is writing a book about the affair at this very moment in which he talks learnedly about something called mass hysteria: they all got each other worked up about nothing much. I can imagine what Mrs Thornton would have to say about that. And a bit of over-excitement doesn't account for peacocks, Greek temples, and a great deal of very real water.

So this book is to put the professor in his place and tell the story as it happened. From the beginning—insofar as there is a beginning—to the end. If it is the end.

It all started in Tim Thornton's bedroom. At the time, though, you would never have recognised it as a bedroom; there was a construction of steel girders and the beginnings of some walls and a lot of tarpaulin flapping from a scaffolding where one day would be Tim's bedroom window.

An eighteen-year-old boy called Stan was trying to sort out the tarpaulin and wishing it was Saturday afternoon and looking down onto the Thorntons' back garden which was a disagreeable mess of mud and rubble lightly covered in snow.

He said, "Here! Come and have a look at this."

The foreman climbed up the scaffolding to join him. He stared down, and then to right and left, into what would in the fullness of time be the Harveys' back garden and the Spenders' back garden. "Funny thing. Trick of the light."

"Mirage?" suggested Stan.

The foreman gave him a kindly smile. "Mirages, son, are what you get in hot countries. Deserts and that. Not in Oxfordshire in the middle of January."

"It's a pattern," said Stan. "It's regular, see. All them lines and squares. Flower-beds, you'd say."

"Trick of the light," repeated the foreman. "You don't have flower-beds in a field, do you? Agricultural land, this was, until it was sold to the developers." Nevertheless, he continued to stare down at the arrangement of interconnecting squares and oblongs and triangles and half-circles that was lightly etched upon the snowy ground, vanishing here and there under a cement mixer or heap of bricks or pegged-out foundations of a house. "Tighten those bolts, son," he said. "We'll take the tea-break soon—it's enough to make you weep, this weather." He climbed slowly down to ground level and stood looking around for a moment. The pattern, if pattern it were, had vanished entirely. "Trick of the light," he muttered, and stumped off to slap some cement around in the Harveys' sitting room. Up aloft, Stan whistled unmelodiously, and when he looked down again, the squares and oblongs were no longer quite so evident, and presently melted away altogether, along with the snow that was rusting into mud.

Most of the housing estate was finished by early summer. A dozen or so houses remained in a skeletal state, and there was still a good deal by way of mud and concrete mixers and gently panting lorries to irritate those who had already moved into the completed houses. The shopping centre opened in July—though this was perhaps an overblown expression for one chemist, a butcher, a small supermarket and a do-it-yourself shop.

The Thorntons moved in two days before Tim's eleventh birthday. He thought—correctly, as it turned out—that this was a bad plan, in that it would undoubtedly take his mother's mind off interesting matters like birthday cakes and a special dinner. In the event, the dinner was provided by Tim's grandfather and was more than adequate, but the cake, as he had feared, was a bought one and on the small side. These problems, though, were pushed out of his mind by the general flurry and commotion of the removal and such diversions as breakages, wardrobes entertainingly stuck on the stairs and out-of-the-ordinary meals at peculiar times. By the morning of the second day, Tim was busily taking stock of the new surroundings: casing the joint.

The house was straightforward enough: it was just a house. So were those to the right and left and those on the other side of the road. The garden was a depressing vista of brown earth scattered with stones and bits of brick. So was the next door one, visible through various cracks in the fence. The housing estate roads were fairly traffic free, had some quite stimulating ups and downs and would do nicely for biking. Great Maxton, the small town on the edge of which the estate had been built, was about ten minutes' walk away and not all that promising. It probably didn't even have a football team, and the only cinema had been showing the same film, by the look of it, for several years. On the other hand, there was Tim's grandfather.

Tim's grandfather had been living in Great Maxton for a long time and was the principal reason why the Thorntons were moving there. To be near my wife's father, said Mr Thornton, now he's getting on a bit. To keep an eye on Dad, said Mrs Thornton darkly.

Grandpa was a widower, Grandma having died a few years ago. Tim was extremely fond of him. Nothing surprised Grandpa, very few things upset him, and he had the most admirable ideas about how life should be arranged. He and Tim shared an intense, and, as they felt, professional interest in food. Indeed much of Tim's serious eating was done at Grandpa's. Grandpa's meals were inventive, prolonged, unpredictable and liable to send the average mother into a nervous breakdown. There might be, say, an all-fried occasion of steak and chips followed by bacon, sausages and mushrooms topped off by the odd beefburger. Or, if Grandpa felt in a different mood, it might be a puddings-only day when chocolate mousse would be followed by treacle tart followed by bananas smothered in cream. When in a poetic frame of mind, Grandpa would spend happy hours in the kitchen experimenting with combinations of meringue, raspberry jam, flaked chocolate and vanilla ice-cream, or pondering the possibilities of a marriage of peanut butter and bubble and squeak. When Grandma was alive nothing of this kind had been allowed; Grandpa had eaten what Tim's mother called a balanced diet and Tim and Grandpa called standard nosh. Nowadays, after a particularly creative menu, Grandpa would cast guilty glances at the photo on the mantelpiece from which Grandma reproachfully observed these goings-on. "She was a wonderful woman, your grandmother," he would say. "One of the best. Finest wife a man could wish for. Didn't do to cross her where domestic matters were concerned, mind. She liked things just so." He would push his moulting slippers under the chair, adjust a toppling pile of old newspapers, sweep tobacco ash under the rug and close the door to the kitchen, from which drifted lingering fumes of fried onion and Christmas pudding.

Grandpa's other interest was his garden, in which flowers of the most amazing size and colour blazed away at those of his competitors next door and over the road. Grandpa liked a display; he grew things for bigness and brightness. He also grew vegetables which he did not eat ("Rabbit-food," he would say, depositing a brimming basket of beans, peas and lettuce in his daughter's kitchen), but which were clearly essential to a man of creative inclinations who liked to show off his gardening capabilities. Grandpa's ranks of onions and cabbages marched with a military precision up and down his sloping garden, his runner beans surged up their poles and exploded from the top in leafy profusion, his lettuces positively crackled with well-being.

Grandpa's house was only a few minutes from the Thorntons' new home. Clearly Tim would be spending a good deal of time there. Of more immediate concern, though, was the matter of the neighbours.

A neighbour, of course, is not a person that you have chosen in any way. Neither, for that matter, are mothers or fathers or brothers or sisters, but they have a curious knack of seeming to have been chosen: exasperating as they may be at times, one usually ends up reckoning that they are preferable to anyone else's, by and large and on the whole, and with a few reservations. But neighbours are another matter and in Tim's experience could often readily be exchanged for a different lot. So it was with interest and not a little suspicion that he investigated the Harveys through a crack in the fence, on the morning after the move.

They also appeared to be very recently moved. There was an atmosphere of unsettlement about both the house and what passed for a garden. Tim observed their comings and goings and made an assessment. Mother, nondescript, could be fussy (something to do with her hair and the kind of shoes she wore). Father, much like any father. Girl, aged ten or thereabouts, short brown hair, incredibly dirty jeans (good sign), many scratches on one arm (interesting—recent encounter with a tiger, perhaps?), spectacles with one cracked glass, and evidently called Jane since that was what everyone kept bawling at her. Small fry by way of one baby in pram (yelling its head off) and something a bit bigger at the moment sitting in a pile of dirt contentedly sucking a snail shell. Tim hoped the snail shell was empty. Well, that was those neighbours, then.

On the other side was a couple without any children and a distinctly prim outlook on life which Tim observed with disquiet. Their house already bloomed with frilly net curtains, a chiming front door bell, an imitation well in the front garden and an artificial lamp-post cemented into the front path. Much car-washing and polishing of windows went on. They were the sort of people, Tim knew, who would object to noise, footballs flying over fences and accidents with water-pistols. They were called Mr and Mrs Spender. Tim gave them placating smiles every time he saw them, to pave the way for future difficulties.

It seemed more likely, on balance, that what you might call a working relationship would be achieved with the Harveys. And indeed by dinner-time that day Tim's mother and Mrs Harvey had met outside their respective garages and reached agreement on a wide matter of subjects such as the inadequacies of the so-called shopping centre, the beauty and charm of Mrs Harvey's baby (an appalling brat, in Tim's opinion) and the undesirability of Tim and Jane being allowed to climb the vast and spreading tree which occupied an island of ground at the junction of two streets just opposite their houses. It was a fine branchy tree, curious in appearance and somehow uneasy in its present surroundings of neat boxy new houses, rather as though it had been left over from something else, and was resolutely making the best of the situation. Tim already had designs on it, and it was typical of his mother's quickness of wit to have rumbled this and got herself an ally in Mrs Harvey even before Tim had made a move. Mrs Thornton was a very sharp lady; she could seldom be outmanoeuvred. She stood shoulder to shoulder with Jane's mother on the garden path and a patter went to and fro from one to the other, as neat as you like, just as though they'd been rehearsing it for years, about how you might fall ten feet onto that concrete and look at those nasty jagged bits and I wouldn't be surprised if some of those branches were rotten. It was a polished performance, to give credit where credit was due.

Jane's reaction was surprising. Instead of disputing the matter she shrugged her shoulders and summoned Tim round to the back of the house. There, she said belligerently, "If we had've done that tree, I'd 've got further up it than you." This statement silenced Tim for a moment, being difficult at first to unravel and flagrantly unfair when you had done so. When he had recovered, they had an argument which raged the length and breadth of the Harveys' garden for some twenty minutes or so, at the end of which they found, somewhat to their surprise, that they were firm friends. After that they did some mutual showing-off by way of gymnastics and bike-riding and anything else that came to mind, during which Jane cracked the other glass of her spectacles and acquired a whole new crop of scratches and bruises. It was not so much that she was clumsy as that she was clearly some kind of natural disaster area. If there was a nail to be trodden on, Jane trod on it; if there was a thorn to get stuck on, Jane got stuck on it; if there was a hard bit of ground to land on, Jane landed on it. She paid not the slightest attention to any of this.

In the matter of personal relationships, Tim had always believed in straightforward no-nonsense reactions. Jane would do, he reckoned. Indeed, he would probably take her to see his grandfather, which was the highest compliment he could pay to anyone.

Later that day Mr Thornton and Mr Harvey made contact. They emerged simultaneously from their back doors and first of all pretended not to see each other in the curious way that grown-up people sometimes do, and then had a little exploratory skirmish about the weather, both of them looking as though they were about to move off to do something more important at any moment, and then settled down to a long shirt-sleeved natter over the garden fence. Jane and Tim, who were both worn out by now—the opening rounds of a friendship can be a very exhausting business—lay on their backs recovering their energies and occasionally listening. Not that the conversation was very interesting; their fathers were discussing methods of laying a lawn and plans for tree-planting and all the things that had been done or left undone by the builders in the way of badly-fitting floor-boards and lack of power sockets. Jane said suddenly, "When I put the light on in my room there's a smell of fruit cake cooking."

Her father gave her a look of irritation. Mr Thornton smiled indulgently in the way that people often do at other people's children. To begin with, Mrs Thornton, who had come out to join them, said, "I expect it's just the new wiring, dear, or the plaster drying out." She then eyed Jane with some horror and began to murmur things about disinfectant and bandages, as indeed she well might. Jane's father, who was presumably so used to Jane's battle-scarred appearance that he no longer saw it, gave her another look of irritation and said that he didn't know how he was going to make a go of this garden with his lot chewing it up all the time. Tim's father made noises of sympathy and agreement.

"And when you put the telly on," continued Jane, "there's a noise like a lot of people doing a lot of washing-up."

"The reception's not good," said Mr Thornton. "Very poor. We're hardly getting BBC2 at all." He moved down the fence with Mr Harvey, to inspect the view from the end of the gardens, which looked out onto open country. Tim and Jane, indeed, had already made several sorties into this promising landscape, and had tried to make friends with some rather unforthcoming cows in the adjacent field. Mrs Thornton went inside again, having instructed Tim that supper was just about ready and he was to come in for it within five minutes.

Tim said to Jane, "Does it honestly?"

"Does it what?"

"The telly. Do that."

"Yes," she said. She didn't sound particularly interested. It struck Tim that Jane, like his grandfather, was probably the sort of person who is unsurprised by things.

"Can you tell me next time it's doing it?"

Jane shrugged. She got up, brushed some of the dirt off

herself, not very effectively, squinted at Tim through the shattered and murky lenses of her spectacles and said, " 'Bye. See you."

"See you," replied Tim.

He went indoors and ate a rather boring supper. Then he watched the telly for a while. There was nothing in any way out of the ordinary about it except that the reception was indeed very bad. From time to time there was an impression of quite unconnected shapes and scenes flitting across the familiar faces of newsreaders or the frantic goings-on in some drama series. His mother kept popping up and down in exasperation to twiddle the knobs. His father, upstairs, was putting up shelves in the bathroom in an atmosphere of mounting fury. He was not very good at that kind of thing. After a particularly devastating clatter and outburst of distress, Tim and his mother went up and found him staring disconsolately at a wall pockmarked with holes. Mrs Thornton made soothing sounds. Her husband glared once more at the wall, flung his tools into a piece of sacking and went downstairs, ordering Tim to bed as he went as though this in some way relieved his feelings. Tim, who knew potential trouble when he saw it, decided it would be more sensible to go than put up a fight.

He lay in bed and went through some ideas for menus that he was intending to discuss with Grandpa. He thought it highly probable that Jane would turn out to be a serious eater too, in which case it might be possible to have a party. Three makes a better party than two. Tim and his grandfather were restricted when it came to party-giving since Mr and Mrs Thornton drew the line at Grandpa's ordinary meals let alone one of his full-scale three-star all-stops-out party meals. The neighbours, too, had taken to declining politely.

He thought about fried egg sandwiches and chocolate layer cake. He heard his parents go to bed. There was silence. Occasionally the house sighed and creaked, as houses do at night, except that this one seemed to do it rather more than most. You'll get settlement, the builders' man had said, bound to with a new construction. Tim wished it wouldn't be quite so energetic about its settling. He thought about nothingness, or at least a field and grass and air, and this nothingness being filled by a house and people where no house had been, indeed lots of houses and people, Thorntons and Harveys and Spenders and so forth, and how curious this was and whether the nothingness, or at least the field and the grass and whatnot, went on being there in a funny way. And in the middle of these rather confused thoughts he turned over, buried his face in the pillow and went fast asleep.

CHAPTER 2

Over the next few weeks the new estate took on a more established look. Lawns arrived, sometimes instantly, as seed grew and flushed the raw earth gardens with green. Trees were planted, infant trees bravely fluttering a few leaves and large labels to tell you what they were. Window-boxes appeared, and dustbins and cats and dogs and lawn-mowers and the milkman and the postman and cars and prams. At the far end of the estate, the brick outlines of more houses rose from the muddy ground, and the lorries continued to come and go and the cement-mixers to rattle and roll. People learned each other's names; likes and dislikes were formed. It was a place.

It was, indeed, Charstock. The Charstock Estate, to be precise, but in no time everyone was referring to it as Charstock. One of the Great Maxton bus routes was diverted to pass through it and thereupon the place officially existed, on the bus time-table. The name had been selected by the man from Great Maxton District Council, many months ago now, as he pored over the map with the man from the firm which was building the houses, Stagg & Co. "What's this about 'site of Charstock Park'?" asked the man from Stagg's. The council man shook his head vaguely and said he understood there'd been some big house there that was knocked down a hundred years or so ago, after a fire.

"Ah," said the man from Stagg's. "That adds up. Fearful lot of stone around, the men are having a spot of bother with it. How about Charstock Estate, then? Sounds all right." So Charstock Estate it was, and then they moved on to the trickier matter of naming the different roads in the estate, which soon had them stumped, both being a little short on imagination. In the end they divided the task between them, and half the roads were named after members of the council man's family and half after the family of the man from Stagg's, who had an Italian grandmother, thus explaining how Tim's road came to be called Gianetti Avenue, a flight of fancy that has mildly puzzled people ever since.

It had no very distinctive air about it. It was much like anywhere, truth to tell; you could have found similar houses with similar cars parked outside them from east to west and from north to south. Such distinction as there was arose, as it frequently does, from people. In no time at all each family had made its presence felt in some way or other, whether it was by an imitation well in the front garden like the Spenders, or a tangle of bikes flung down on the doorstep by the four sons of the Rutters in Macpherson Close (the man from the council was of Scottish ancestry), or by the various caravans, boats and so forth which adorned the front gardens of other houses, defining the families' interests and generally cluttering the landscape.

The Harveys' house was distinguished by Jane's bike, which was as battered in appearance as its owner and usually head-down in Mr Harvey's newly-planted rose-bed. The Thorntons' boasted a peculiarly disagreeable imitation wrought-iron plant-holder which had been given them as a house-moving present by Mr Thornton's mother and had to be displayed lest she pass by unexpectedly. Since it was made of plastic and presumably indestructible, they were becoming resigned to living behind it for ever.

Much competition went into the matter of gardens. Most people were quick to tackle the forbidding blanks of earth left by the builders and vied with one another in the laying of lawns, marking out of flower-beds and acquiring of plants and trees. Mr Harvey announced that he was going in for vegetables and spent much time digging, re-digging and marking out rows with pieces of string. Tim, who reckoned himself an expert on vegetable-growing at least in a second-hand sense since he had so frequently watched his grandfather, sat astride the fence and offered advice which Mr Harvey endured with clenched teeth. The larger of the two Harvey babies crawled all over the rows of seeds as soon as they were planted.

Tim took Jane to see Grandpa. They had tea there. Jane ate more tea than anyone and Grandpa was favourably impressed. "Nice lass, that," he said to Tim, confidentially. "Got the right ideas." Jane, at the kitchen table, worked her way through her fourth slice of cake and then had to go and sit down quietly for a bit to recover. Later, they did a conducted tour of Grandpa's garden and admired his mammoth roses, his explosive hollyhocks and his record-breaking sunflowers. Grandpa's house was on the outskirts of Great Maxton and the garden overlooked Charstock and the surrounding countryside. The children climbed on the wall and tried to pick out their own houses, unsuccessfully since at this range the housing estate looked like a series of matchboxes laid out in tidy lines and curves. In the end they managed to pin-point their road because of the big tree opposite their houses, the one they were not allowed to climb. "Turkey oak," said Grandpa. "Unusual sort of a tree to be stuck in a field like that, I used to notice it. Very old, I should imagine." The tree, from there, dwarfed the surrounding houses and gave an even stronger impression of determined survival.

The following Sunday Grandpa paid a return visit. He spent the day at Tim's house, as he did from time to time, and trundled round the estate making critical remarks about people's gardens. After dinner he inspected the Thorntons' garden and looked over the fence into the Harveys', where Mr Harvey was admiring his newly-sprouting rows of vegetables. There were greetings and introductions. Grandpa looked speculatively at Mr Harvey's achievement. "Ah," he said. "Box. Interesting. You don't see that grown a lot."

Mr Harvey stared at his plants. "French beans. Suttons' Majestic. Long-pod."

Grandpa smiled kindly. "Box, I'm afraid."

Mr Harvey strode off to his newly-erected toolshed and returned with a crumpled seed packet, which he handed to Grandpa, who examined it and gave it back. "I daresay. But what you've got coming up there is a box hedge."

"I'll complain to the manufacturers," said Mr Harvey angrily. After a moment he added, in rather plaintive tones, "What do you do with a box hedge?"

"You square it off with a few more and make a bed," said Grandpa. "Put roses in the middle and that kind of thing. Very classy. Mind, I don't know about box in a garden like this, it's more a stately-home kind of arrangement. Ambitious. Still, it would be stylish, I'll say that." He surveyed Mr Harvey's garden for a few moments and then wandered indoors, leaving Mr Harvey gazing in bewilderment at his row of sturdy little plants.

After tea they watched a bit of a television series about

cops and robbers somewhere in America. Grandpa, who did not own a television set and had a low opinion of the whole process but nonetheless various ideas upon how it should be done (as he did on everything), sat making loud remarks. "That fellow needs a haircut," he'd say. Or, "I could have told them there was a bloke hiding behind that door, you could spot that a mile off." Or, "She got what was coming to her, that woman, and she wants to get herself a decent dress to wear while she's about it." The children, who were used to this, paid no attention.

Mrs Thornton, maddened, would allow herself to be drawn into involved explanations and discussions which ended up drowning the programme for everybody. In the end, as usual, she huddled in her chair saying, "Oh, ssh, Dad," at intervals.

"Keep your hair on, Mary," said Grandpa equably. "You want to look at this kind of thing with a clear eye, that's all. Raise the odd question."

At supper-time, Mr Thornton came in and said, "You've got Harvey next door properly steamed up about this box hedge or whatever, Dad."

"Can't help that. A box hedge is a box hedge."

"It's a rather odd business," said Mr Thornton. "He swears blue there were bean seeds in that packet. No possible mistake."

Grandpa shrugged. "Nature goes its own way."

"Oh, come on, Dad," said Mrs Thornton. "Nature doesn't suddenly start growing a box hedge where someone planted beans."

Grandpa heaved himself to his feet. "I'll be off home now, it's gone nine. Don't you underrate nature, my girl. Too many people think in straight lines, that's the trouble. Good-night, then."

Tim and Jane spent much time together. Like all friendships, theirs was subject to ups and downs. When there was a serious down period they had a good fight—usually verbal but occasionally physical—and then made it up again almost immediately. They found that the two of them together were very much better at devising ways of passing the time, and very satisfactory ways at that, than just one would have been. Tim was best at having ideas; Jane was best at carrying them out. On the other hand, Jane was capable of sudden flashes of inspiration which could make or save a situation. She was also very good at managing the mothers, usually by a system of docile and helpful behaviour which would be a lead-up to asking for something not usually allowed or getting permission to do something not usually approved of.

She appeared at Tim's front door one morning. "We're going to take the shopping lists and do all the supermarket shopping for my mum. And yours."

"Why?" said Tim.

"Because then this afternoon we're going to ask if we can take bikes and an enormous picnic tea and go by ourselves down to the river."

I should add, in case the two of them seem to you at this point somewhat calculating, not to say of downright bad character, that they were both capable of behaving quite otherwise, and performing such acts of martyrdom as shopping or washing up for no other reason than sheer good nature. It was just that from time to time a little cunning seemed no bad thing.

Charstock now boasted a greengrocer as well as the supermarket, butcher, chemist and do-it-yourself shop. The shopping centre was always busy, littered with prams and mothers. Jane and Tim, wheeling the old push-chair in which they were going to transport things, were therefore not particularly surprised to see quite a crowd outside the small supermarket. But when they reached it they realised that all was not quite as it should be this morning. On the door of the shop was a large hand-written sign saying TEMPORARILY CLOSED OWING TO FLOODING. The door, however, was open, and the manageress, a normally brisk lady now in a state of some excitement, was confronting her frustrated customers.

". . . Three inches deep in the stockroom and still pouring into the shop when I came in this morning. Wading in it, we were. I said to Chrissie, it's no good, we'll have to get the fire brigade, this isn't something we can cope with ourselves, and then it started going down, just like that. Kind of emptied away again. We're nearly dried out now, but the mess! Most of the dry goods in the stockroom we've lost, the cereals and that. It'll be after dinner before we're cleared up." Indeed, the shop, seen beyond her, was something of a shambles, with mud and wet all over the floor and the shelves disarranged.

At this point a car arrived.

"Here's the man from the builders," said the manageress threateningly. "About time too. I've told them I want to know what's what. Did they build this place on a river? That's what I want to know!"

The crowd, including Jane and Tim, listened with pleasure as she embarked on an interestingly aggressive conversation with the new arrival.

"Burst pipe," said the builders' man. "That'll be the trouble. Soon put that right."

The manageress retorted that there was no burst pipe.

"Come now," said the builders' man. "Must be. Let's have a dekko. You don't get water coming up and going down again out of nowhere. There's not even been any rain."

The two of them went into the shop to carry on the dispute.

In the early afternoon the shop reopened and the children were able to do the shopping. The manageress was still holding forth to anyone who would listen.

"And I said to him, all right you show me the burst pipe. Where is it, then? He was on his hands and knees half an hour before he'd give in. Went on insisting there was this burst pipe. Then he started on something changing the water table. I don't know about any water tables, I said, but I want this sorted out once and for all. I'm not having this shop flooded again."

The local paper, the next week, carried a small news item about the incident. It referred to the fact that the Charstock Estate had been built on the site of a seventeenth-century mansion and its park, Charstock House, which had been burnt down and then demolished in 1800. It also quoted an anonymous person employed by the development company who said there had been a lot of trouble of one kind and another during the construction of the houses and the shopping centre. He mentioned mysterious appearances and disappearances of water. He said the workmen had been hindered by the remains of walls which had forced them to stop work but that when contractors had been brought in to remove the walls they could no longer be found. He said from time to time there had been curious smells. He said he reckoned the place had a jinx on it. The managing director of the building company wrote an angry letter to the paper the following week denying it all.

But Jane and Tim were not much concerned with this.

They did vaguely hear their parents talking about it, in the way that one does vaguely hear parents. Later on the afternoon of the flooding, they did indeed get permission to take a picnic down to the river and spent a memorable couple of hours there during which Jane ripped her T-shirt from top to bottom on a fence and added to the already impressive series of scars down one leg. It had been a very energetic picnic.

On the way back they called in on Grandpa to tell him about it, and also about the flooding at the supermarket. They also passed on to him a useful tip about corned beef and fried onion sandwiches in which he was indeed much interested. The matter of the supermarket afforded him a certain malevolent pleasure. Grandpa, who took shopping almost as seriously as eating and regarded the selection and purchase of food as something that should be done slowly, carefully and, if possible, over a long discussion with a friendly shop assistant, did not care for supermarkets. "Everybody shoving each other with wire prams. Everything done up in plastic. Not a decent banger in the place. Expect you to line up like a lot of sheep. So they got flooded out, did they? Serve 'em right."

Having paid little attention to what was said about the piece in the local paper, Jane and Tim paid equally little to the comments that residents of the estate were exchanging about the various shortcomings of the houses. When your immediate interests are food and how best to spend the day—it was the school holidays so there was a great deal of day to be spent—the grumblings of parents about electricity failures, uneven walls, doors that won't open or close properly and erratic telephones are of no great consequence. Eventually, however, it was borne in on the children that there was more adult fuss and bother than usual in these parts. And from time to time you could see their point. Tim, coming into the kitchen one morning, was assailed by the most pungent and indeed appetising smell.

He paused to consider it. Bacon? No, not quite, though in that line, possibly. Roast beef? Yes, that was a bit closer. He was filled with a nice warm glow of anticipation.

"What's for dinner, Mum?"

Mrs Thornton was squatting in front of the washing-machine. As he spoke she got up and clouted the thing in fury. The machine rocked and juddered to a halt.

"You shouldn't do that," said Tim piously. "You'll make it go wrong."

His mother glared at him. "It already has gone wrong. For the third time this week. You put the load in and two minutes later there's this fearful smell and it's packed up again."

Tim's spirits fell. Not dinner, then. He studied the machine, which studied him back with a vast enigmatic eye behind which slopped his football jersey and innumerable socks. "Better get the washing-machine man," he said helpfully. Mrs Thornton gave him a baleful look and went to the telephone.

The engineer's arrival coincided with that of Grandpa, who had come to borrow an extra saucepan for an ambitious cookery experiment. He followed the engineer into the kitchen, sniffing appreciatively. "Venison," he said. "Very nice too. Done with a drop of red wine, if I'm not mistaken."

Mrs Thornton ignored him. She said to the engineer, "You see?"

The engineer squatted down and began unscrewing things. "Not to worry. It'll be the heater's blown a fuse, I daresay. Or the pump's failed. Or the drum's come loose. Soon put that right."

"You'd want some red currant jelly with it," continued Grandpa reflectively. "And something lightish after. A sorbet, perhaps. A lemon sorbet. And then maybe a really good cheese to finish off."

The engineer was fiddling about with the machine's intestines. "The smell I can't quite account for, I must say. Overheating, probably."

"Last time," said Mrs Thornton, "it was quite different. You'd have sworn there was a fruit cake cooking."

"With brandy?" enquired Grandpa eagerly.

The engineer fixed the back on the machine once more and switched on. Instantly the room was filled with a further injection of juicy, mouth-watering smell.

"Smashing," said Grandpa. "Lovely job. There's been someone that knows their stuff working on that lot—you can practically see the gravy."

Mrs Thornton turned a steely eye on him. "You'll find the paper through in the sitting room, Dad. Why don't you have a bit of a rest before you go back?"

After a quarter of an hour or so the smell was somewhat dimmed and the machine was working again. The engineer, however, was dissatisfied. "The truth is," he said, piling tools into his bag, "I couldn't find a darn thing wrong with it. Can't understand. Don't see why it's going again now, either."

Mrs Thornton, however, was too relieved to enter into a discussion about it. The engineer departed, shaking his head. Tim's football jersey and the socks obediently rotated and everyone dismissed the matter, except Grandpa, who had been stirred into a long and precise recollection of venison he had eaten in Scotland in the dim and distant past. Jane, arriving in the middle, said, "What's venison?"

"Deer," said Mrs Thornton. "Not a thing I'd fancy myself."

"Cruel," remarked Jane, after a pause for reflection.

This prompted a short argument between Jane and Tim about why and if it should be more cruel to eat deer than cows or pigs, which was eventually ended by Mrs Thornton pointing out that hardly anyone did so nowadays anyway.

"When did they, then?" asked Jane.

Mrs Thornton was vague on the matter, but Grandpa reckoned it would have gone on a good bit in the old days. "Only for the nobs, mind," he added. "The rich folk. People with parks and that to keep them in."

Later on Jane and Tim walked back with Grandpa to keep him company, and Grandpa told them a good story about something that happened to him once a long time ago. The story got wilder and wilder and more and more improbable, and they both suspected the truth of it, but this was really neither here nor there since it was a good story anyway. Most of Grandpa's stories were like that. Mrs Thornton, on these occasions, would look at him through narrowed eyes and say, "Now then, Dad, you don't expect us to believe that, do you?" and Grandpa would reply, "You must suit yourself, my dear." The children, doing precisely that, listened appreciatively. They parted from him at the garden gate and set off home, laden with a carrier bag of lettuces and beans.

They walked back in silence, having nothing particular to say. Jane's face, behind a lather of freckles and a new scratch across one cheek, was blank; in fact, she was in the middle of a very exciting story she was telling herself. The story had been going on for several weeks and involved everything from piracy to the exploration of the Amazon to a famous battle in which Jane was both generals. In fact, Jane was all the characters, which meant a good deal of dashing around and changes of costume. At this precise moment she was a stunningly beautiful lady being attacked by a highwayman and rescued by a gentleman of amazing courage and resourcefulness, and of course she was all three of them which meant concentrating hard. Hence the blankness of her expression.

Tim, on the other hand, was looking at the landscape. They were walking down the hill from Great Maxton to Charstock and the estate lay just below and in front of them, with the houses wheeling out from the shopping centre which was in a dip in the middle. Beyond and around were fields, dotted with grazing cows and lined with trees. There were a lot of trees; some of them, Tim noticed, were neatly grouped. They seemed to have been arranged, rather then just to have grown. He thought again about houses being dumped down—or mushrooming up, whichever way you looked at it—where no houses had been, ousting cows and trees or other houses or anything else that had been there before. Of course, that happened all over the place, and always had done, for ever and ever. It was interesting, when you thought about it; perhaps, occasionally, what had been there before might resent being wiped out like that. He thought of something Mrs Spender had said over the fence to his mother: "There's something about these houses, they don't seem to settle down." He thought also of the remark quoted in the local paper: "That estate's got a jinx on it."

CHAPTER 3

I suppose that in any series of events, any history, there is a point at which things gather speed, when the pace is stepped up, when there is a sense of being swept onwards, willy-nilly, by what is happening. This is certainly how it was in the Charstock affair. Afterwards, it was possible to see such things as Mr Harvey's box hedge and the curious behaviour of Mrs Thornton's washing-machine, not to mention the flooding of the supermarket, as the opening moves in the drama. At the time, they seemed merely odd little happenings probably of no great significance. Later, they could be seen in their true colours. The professor from the university, who is going round interviewing people about it right now, has made a sort of chart with much fancy mathematical stuff and some improbable language. Whether this is meant to make things clearer is not entirely apparent. So far as we are concerned, he is best left to it; we shall get on with the story as it happened, and the point at which things began to happen rather faster.

Which was the point at which the Spenders' new greenhouse was delivered and the first brick walls appeared.

It was a Sunday. The Spenders' greenhouse, an affair of boarding and steel frames and glass panels stacked in a lorry, had been delivered on the Saturday, and Mr Spender had spent much of the day assembling it. From time to time he seemed in some distress, standing back to stare and mutter, and continuing well into the dusk so that it was almost dark when the sounds of hammering ceased.

On the following morning Grandpa came over for a late breakfast and to spend the day. He and Tim were alone in the kitchen, finishing off, when they looked out of the window to see something going on in the Spenders' garden. Various people were gathered: namely, the Harveys, the Spenders and Tim's own parents. Tim and Grandpa went out to see what was up.

Everyone was staring at the greenhouse. Mr Spender, in shirt sleeves, very hot and bothered, was arguing with his wife. "I followed the instructions to the letter. I did exactly what the booklet said. It was going up nicely, I thought, though there were one or two things that seemed a bit funny. And then I came out this morning and now look at it!"

"That's not what we ordered," stormed Mrs Spender. "Whoever saw a greenhouse like that! It looks like a . . . a . . ."

There was a silence.

"A Greek temple," suggested Tim.

"Right," said Mrs Spender, who was close to tears. "It's like those things on travel brochures, for Rhodes or wherever. It's ridiculous! What we asked for out of the catalogue was a nine by six cedar frame greenhouse with louvre windows and low level staging. What we've got is . . ."

"What you've got," said Grandpa, "is an eighteenth-century garden folly with classical pediment and Corinthian pillars. Very nice too."

Mr Spender was now stamping up and down and declaring that someone had been tampering with it during the night. "Some joker must have come in and switched around all that stuff I put up and . . ." His voice trailed away; it did not, indeed, sound a likely theory.

"It's unusual," said Mrs Thornton doubtfully.

"It's conspicuous," wept Mrs Spender. "People will say we're making a display of ourselves. I wanted a cedar greenhouse for my tomatoes. How can I grow tomatoes in that? Trust you to make a hash of it, Jim. You never were anything of a handyman."

Other people, anxious to avert an ugly domestic scene, broke in with suggestions about what might be done. Mr Thornton fancied glazing the front in and trying a vine up it. Mrs Harvey thought it would be nice as a summerhouse with one of those upholstered swing seats and a wrought-iron table. Mr Spender had switched to another tack and was in favour of taking legal action against the manufacturers. He and his wife continued to argue. Everybody else drifted away, though not before agreeing that it was all a bit of an odd business. Back in the Thorntons' kitchen the matter was pursued.

"Spender ordered the wrong stuff, that's all," said Mr Thornton.

Mrs Thornton pointed out that manufacturers of cedar greenhouses don't also sell replicas of Greek temples. Normally.

Tim and Jane were finishing off overlooked bits of breakfast. Tim was still thinking deeply about the whole matter. He had this hazy sensation that there was a puzzle somewhere . . . just out of reach . . . that you only had to make sense of something, catch hold of it. . . .

Jane said, "It changed in the night."

"How could it, dear?" said Mrs Thornton kindly. "No, I expect what happened was that . . ."

Jane, through a mouthful of toast, continued. "I saw it when I went to bed and it was what they said. A cedar frame whatsit. Then I woke up very early in the morning and looked out to see if it was the morning or it wasn't and there it was. Like it is now."

"Well, I must say on the face of it one has to admit that is what *seems* to have happened," said Mr Thornton with a little laugh. "But of course it would be absurd to . . ."

Grandpa folded his newspaper over with an explosive noise and looked up. "It reminds me of a time I may not have told you about during the war when I was responsible for the erection of six Nissen huts and during the night . . ."

"Yes, you have, Dad," said Mr and Mrs Thornton simultaneously.

Grandpa gave them a look of suspicion. "Eh? Well, be that as it may, I wouldn't be too hasty in looking for the obvious explanation. It never pays. Would there be a cup of coffee going?" He returned to the newspaper, extracts from which he proceeded to read aloud to anyone handy for the next two hours.

Jane and Tim went outside to get started on whatever they were going to do that day. From time to time Mr Spender emerged from his house and glared balefully at the construction in his garden, which sat there serenely in the sunshine, looking quite settled and, one had to admit, a great deal more elegant than the Spenders' house. Or, indeed, the Thorntons' or anyone else's. It was rather hard to tell what it was made of. It was a nice sparkling white and appeared to be stone, though in the circumstances this did not seem possible. The four pillars were most gracefully fluted and above them was a triangular space enclosing a very agreeable carving of ladies in floaty clothes passing ropes of flowers to each other. The children thought it really rather too good for the Spenders.

The matter of the greenhouse left everyone feeling curiously unsettled. Uneasy, even. Word of it soon got around and during the day a number of people drifted past the Spenders' house, trying to look as though they had been going that way anyway and casting inquisitive glances through into the garden. Mrs Spender remained behind her frilly curtains, sulking. Mr Spender emerged from time to time to stare at his new possession in what seemed a mixture of despair and bewilderment.

That night, when there was a full moon, it looked even more emphatic. It stood there shining, quite eclipsing the surrounding houses.

The television was particularly indistinct that evening. Several times Tim could have sworn that the shadowy figure of a *man*—a man in some kind of old-fashioned gear and smoking a very long-stemmed pipe—appeared to stump across the screen. It must, of course, be an illusion, but it was a remarkably convincing one.

Two days later the appearance of the first brick wall became publicly known.

Grandpa had been down to return the borrowed saucepan and had invited Tim and Jane to come back with him for tea, an invitation that was accepted with enthusiasm. They were walking along McAndrew Way when they were halted by the sound of raised voices in an adjoining garden. Voices raised in anger. Two men were standing in the garden, in furious confrontation. One of them, catching sight of Grandpa, beckoned. "Just a minute—I'd like to put a question to you."

The garden held a newly-turfed lawn bordered with flower-beds in which small plants were arranged with mathematical accuracy. Young trees, strapped to posts, were planted at the four corners of the lawn. Across the middle of it, though, there straggled an untidy line of crumbling bricks.

"What," said the man, pointing, "would you call that?"

Grandpa considered. "I'd say that was a brick wall. Foundations of, at any rate."

"Right," said the man with satisfaction. "Now Mr Cramp here from Stagg & Co. won't have it that that is a brick wall. Mr Cramp says there's no brick walls here as far as Stagg's is concerned. Mr Cramp says that brick wall does not exist."

"I never went as far as to say . . ." began Mr Cramp.

"Would anyone in their right mind," continued the owner of the garden, still addressing Grandpa, "lay a lawn on top of a brick wall? I ask you that. I'm telling you that wall has risen up from nowhere. First there was this yellow mark where the grass wouldn't take hold, and then there was this brick wall. And furthermore it's growing. Last week it was one foot two inches. This morning it's one foot seven. Horrabin's the name, by the way."

Grandpa leaned over the fence. "Let's have a look at one of those bricks."

Mr Horrabin prised a brick from the ground and gave it to him. Grandpa turned it over, inspecting it. "This is old brick. Very old. There hasn't been brick like that used for—oh, for a hundred and fifty years and more. Handmade, those bricks are. It's not a smooth mix. That clay was puddled by hand sometime in the eighteenth century. To my mind, anyway."

"And laid on that wall sometime since Monday of last week," said Mr Cramp heavily. "Now, Mr Horrabin, you surely can't expect the company to . . ."

Mr Horrabin glared at him. "I am merely pointing out a few facts to the company. A wall is a fact, isn't it?"

"A wall is a fact," agreed Mr Cramp. "Fair enough. I'm not disputing that. What I am disputing . . ."

"Disputing's not going to sort out this wall," retorted Mr Horrabin. "And sort out this wall's what the company's got to do. This house and this garden were sold to me by the company as a house and a garden. Nothing was said about walls where no walls ought to be. The company's liable, to my mind."

"If it was a question of subsidence, now," began Mr Cramp, "we might take a different view."

"What you've got there," said Grandpa with interest, "is *up*-sidence, more. Very remarkable. One would like to let nature take its course, in a way. See what happens."

"And what about my lawn?" demanded Mr Horrabin.

Grandpa agreed that it wasn't doing the lawn much good.

"And I'll tell you another thing," Mr Horrabin went on, thrusting his face closer to Mr Cramp. "My wife thinks it's starting to come up through the downstairs toilet floor. The lino's splitting."

Eventually Grandpa and the children moved away, leaving the two men still locked in argument. Mr Horrabin wanted the company to pay for the removal of the wall and the re-laying of the lawn. Mr Cramp continued stoutly to deny responsibility, on grounds that shifted from casting doubts on the existence of the wall to dark hints that Mr Horrabin might have built it himself.

Over tea, they discussed the matter.

"He didn't build it himself," said Jane. "That Mr Horrabin. He was too cross about it. And he wasn't a person who'd be that good at pretending."

The others were inclined to agree.

Grandpa divided the last chocolate eclair between them and began to cut the cake. "Lovely mellow colour, old brick. If I were him I'd let it run its course, and grow a peach up it. They can get to six feet and more, those old walls. Kitchen garden wall it looked like to me, just right for fruit. South-facing, too."

"D'you think it would grow to six feet?" said Tim.

Grandpa shrugged. "There's no knowing. I've never seen one behave like that before as it is."

Jane paused in the middle of her slice of cake (one of Grandpa's specialities: walnut and cherry with coffee icing). "The Spenders' greenhouse. This wall. My dad's bean plants. Your mum's washing-machine. The way the televisions go wrong all the time." She ticked off the items on her fingers and went back to her slice of cake.

"I take your point," said Grandpa. "There's something funny going on."

"It's as though," said Tim after a moment, "there was something kind of fighting back. As though something didn't like this estate being built here. As though it was coming up through it."

"Or someone?" suggested Jane.

Grandpa poured himself another cup of tea. "I reckon there's been disturbance. Something or someone's been disturbed and it's making its presence felt. A place is bound to have its feelings, just like a person does. And if you think that's far-fetched then you're one of those that think in straight lines. You want to think flexibly. And never underrate nature."

"Do you think," said Tim carefully, "it's going to be *dangerous*?"

Grandpa pondered for a moment. "Nothing particularly dangerous about a greenhouse. Nor a smell of roast venison. Nor an old brick wall. Interesting, I'd reckon, rather than dangerous. It'll depend a bit how people respond, mind."

He was quite right, of course. Later, much later, they remembered this conversation and Grandpa pointed out with some relish that it was the responses that had caused half the trouble. In a manner of speaking. If people had just sat tight and let things take their course, let the place have its say, as it were, then everything might have been all right.

But I am getting ahead of things.

For the next few days life in Charstock was quiet. Ordinary. On the surface, nothing much happened though, presumably, human nature being what it is, the normal amount of activity was going on by way of rows and reconciliations and hilarity and despair and breakages and burnt toast. But to the casual observer the place might have been asleep, the houses sitting buttoned up in the rather sultry summer weather and the streets empty except for the occasional loitering child or mother with pram.

On Friday two more families discovered brick walls.

The first was at the house on the corner of Gianetti Avenue and McAndrew Way. It slanted across the front path and disappeared under the garage, where it had apparently been unable to surface, re-emerging on the far side to cross the next garden path and turn right into the road. Neighbours came to visit throughout the morning, while the owner of the house, a widowed lady who bred small square white dogs, stood about in perplexity, explaining for the umpteenth time that it had just appeared out of the blue and she didn't see how she was going to get her car over it. Some people brought cameras and took photographs. The small white dogs came out and yapped.

The second wall was rather shorter and less robust. It came up through the pavement on Hammond Drive, where it had had difficulty with the tarmac, and then petered out against the telephone kiosk on the corner which was evidently too much for it altogether.

The widowed lady rang Stagg & Co., who sent Mr Cramp down. Mr Cramp inspected the walls and declined to comment, but later in the day a lorry arrived with three men armed with picks and shovels. The walls—neither of which were more than a few inches high—were demolished and the bricks flung into the back of the lorry. Grandpa, who had been fetched by Tim in order that he shouldn't miss the excitement, watched with disapproval, as did Tim and Jane. Things, they felt, were not being allowed to run their proper course. "They can't take a lot of resistance, those walls," said Grandpa thoughtfully. "See the way that one couldn't manage the pavement. Interesting. Could be they're not at their full strength yet."

The next morning a notice appeared in the window of the supermarket. 'CHARSTOCK RESIDENTS' ASSOCIATION,' it read. 'All are invited to the opening meeting of the Charstock Residents' Association in the Primary School on Thursday 8 August at 7.30. PLEASE DO YOUR BEST TO COME. In view of recent events the formation of a Residents' Association is felt by a number of us to be of urgent importance, both to discuss various incidents on the estate and also to enable us to raise these matters with the development company and with Great Maxton District Council. YOU ARE URGED TO ATTEND!'

"Can children," asked Tim that evening, "go to this meeting they're having?"

"No," replied his parents, both at once.

"I don't see why not."

"I do," said Mr Thornton grimly.

"Are you going?"

"I daresay."

Mrs Thornton said she most certainly was. The washing-machine had been playing up again, performing its cycle in reverse and filling the kitchen with a smell which Grandpa had defined with interest and enthusiasm as mulled wine. Mrs Thornton said that washing-machine had never given a jot of trouble in their old house and she wanted to know just what it was that was wrong with the electricity in these parts that it could play havoc with a perfectly good washing-machine.

They watched the news on television. The set crackled irritatingly until Mr Thornton gave it a bang and then the sound improved but at the expense of the vision, which developed a curious swimming effect, so that the newsreader appeared to be under water. From time to time the whole screen dimmed and shadows fled across it; Tim fancied he could see a lady in a long dress, and then somebody energetically stirring a saucepan, and then once again that portly gentleman smoking a long-stemmed pipe. Indeed, as though to strengthen the illusion, there came at that very moment a most distinct smell of pipe tobacco. Mrs Thornton, sniffing suspiciously, toured the house in search of fire. There was also a distant but infuriating clattering from somewhere within the television, rather as though an army of midgets were washing dishes inside it. Finally Mr Thornton switched it off, saying that the deplorable reception was something else that would have to be brought up at the meeting of the Residents' Association.

CHAPTER 4

"A *museum*?" cried Tim in horror. "An *art gallery*?"

His mother turned a cold eye on him. "And whose birthday treat is it?"

"All right, all right. Yours."

"Precisely," said Mrs Thornton. "Which is why we are not going to a motor-bike scramble or a funfair or an over-crowded beach. We shall go to Oxford and have a restaurant meal that I haven't cooked myself and visit the Ashmolean Museum and maybe have a walk by the river and possibly a look round the shops if I feel inclined. You can ask Jane if she would like to come too," she added, as a concession.

"Is Grandpa?"

"Of course."

Tim perked up. The restaurant part, at least, sounded promising.

Grandpa was in a holiday mood. He loved outings. He had given his daughter as a birthday present an enormous book called *Indonesian Cookery in Full Colour* which he said he would borrow back off her right away if she didn't mind. He sat in the back of the car enjoying the scenery and staring into neighbouring cars every time they stopped at a traffic light. Grandpa found other people intensely interesting; he was the kind of person who strikes up relationships at bus-stops or in shops or anywhere handy. He also liked to speculate about passers-by. Jane and Tim sat on either side of him and entered into the spirit of the thing. "That fellow," said Grandpa, peering into a sleek Jaguar purring beside them at a road-junction, "is up to no good. Drug smuggling, I don't doubt, or terrorism or some such caper. You've only got to look at his tie."

"Really, Dad," exclaimed Mrs Thornton from the front, rising to the bait as usual. "There's absolutely no . . ."

"And that lot"—scrutinising another family outing—"may appear straightforward enough, but I suspect in fact what we've got there is a party of anarchists. There's a look in that woman's eye. . . ."

"What's anarchists?" interrupted Jane.

"Ah," said Grandpa. "Interesting you should ask. Now a long time ago when I was . . ."

The journey passed pleasantly enough.

As did the meal. After a short period for digestion they proceeded to the Ashmolean, a building of Grecian splendour and an atmosphere of seriousness which daunted Tim, who was feeling very full and slightly sleepy. He followed his parents in without enthusiasm, and toured with them a rather repetitive display of Greek statues, a vista of drapery and muscular unclothed arms and legs. Mrs Thornton said she was going upstairs to see the paintings. Grandpa looked at the stairs and said he didn't reckon he'd get up those just at the moment and he'd have a wander round on this floor. The children decided to join him.

They abandoned the statues and went into a room devoted to prehistoric remains. Grandpa, inspecting case after case in which Bronze Age pots were displayed, either in bits or carefully stuck together again, got quite distressed. "Dreadfully inadequate cooking arrangements—no wonder the poor fellows died out." He moved on to the next room and paused before a sign with an arrow which announced a special exhibition called Vanished Landscapes. "How about that?" said Grandpa. "Sounds harmless enough. Shall we give it a try?" The children supposed they might as well.

Vanished Landscapes turned out to be, for the most part, a range of photographs of buildings of agreeable bits of countryside with, beside them, further photographs showing how these things either weren't there any more or had been replaced by multi-storey car parks or coal-mines. Grandpa went round tutting and commenting. He didn't always agree with the exhibition, which seemed to be saying that everything ought to stand still for ever. Once, he found a photograph of a terrace of houses exactly the same, he claimed, as the one in which he had been born and expressed considerable satisfaction at its replacement by a municipal swimming-pool. There was a photograph of people having a good time at the swimming-pool which did indeed seem an improvement on the photograph of the terrace houses, outside which stood children without any shoes, and women wearing aprons and curlers.

Beyond the photographs was a smaller section of the exhibition which was entirely paintings. Large oil paintings of chunks of scenery or, in several instances, enormous houses. The same point was being made: none of these places any longer existed.

Grandpa and the children passed before these without any very intense interest until all of a sudden Jane halted. She was staring at a painting of a large house with a lake in front of it set amid rolling scenery dotted with trees and carefully arranged animals. "Hey," she said. "Look!"

A small gold plaque under the painting read CHARSTOCK PARK, BY J. P. TIMMS (1692–1758). Beside it was the exhibition's label, which said that Charstock House (William Kent) had been destroyed by fire in 1800 and the remains subsequently demolished, and that the gardens and park, a magnificent instance of picturesque landscape gardening by Samuel Stokes, had now completely vanished and indeed had recently been built over. The lake had been drained in the nineteenth century but the depression in the ground made by Samuel Stokes could still be seen as could, from the air, the outlines of his formal garden and parterre behind the site of the house.

"Well, well, *well,*" said Grandpa.

"I know where this depression thing, where the lake was, is," said Jane.

"Under the shopping centre," said Tim.

They looked at each other.

Grandpa stared intently at the painting. "Interesting. Quite remarkably interesting, come to that. Quite extraordinarily interesting."

Some of the animals, on closer inspection, were deer. Others were brown cows, standing around in groups of three. On the lake was a small boat from which a man was fishing. To the right of the house, half concealed among a clump of trees, was a small white building like a Greek temple.

Just like, indeed, the Spenders' greenhouse.

The mansion itself was very large, with a central part also Greekly pillared and roofed, a fine balustraded flight of steps leading to the front door, and adjoining wings at either side forming a kind of courtyard. There were urns upon the front steps and statues here and there. It was all very imposing. A small group of people in eighteenth-century costume stood about outside, evidently admiring their property.

"Hmm," said Grandpa. "Stable block. Orangery. Classical stuff. The works, in fact. The kitchens'll be tucked away out of sight, I don't doubt."

Alongside the painting were two smaller ones. The first was a head and shoulders portrait of an elderly man wearing a powdered wig, white cravat and black jacket. He stared rather menacingly out from the picture, as though he were a person not to be trifled with. The second was of the same man but full-length this time and standing beside a young tree evidently directing the labours of a number of other men who were digging and trundling carts about. He was smoking a long-stemmed white pipe. SAMUEL STOKES, LANDSCAPE GARDENER said the label alongside. In the distance the lake could be seen glinting and the landscape looked curiously bare, as if it had been recently stripped of anything superfluous by way of trees, hedges or other intrusions.

Jane said, "That tree's just like the tree opposite our house. Only smaller."

Grandpa peered. "Quite right. Turkey oak. Fancy that."

Once again, they looked at each other.

At that moment Mr and Mrs Thornton appeared. "*There* you are," said Mrs Thornton. "We've been hunting everywhere. Had enough?"

"Look," said Tim.

His parents moved closer. "Charstock . . ." said Mr Thornton. "Is that anything to do with . . . ?" And then "Isn't that interesting, Mary, that house must have been where the estate is now."

"How extraordinary," said Mrs Thornton. "What a funny coincidence." She looked at the picture and then almost immediately at her watch. "Gracious, half past three already—you know, I think if we're going to get our walk by the river we'll have to move on."

The picture was not referred to again. Tim, nevertheless, kept returning to it in his mind and it was still with him when he went to bed that night: the great sprawling house, the lake, the trees, the temple. And the face of Samuel Stokes, Landscape Gardener, whose powerful personality seemed scornfully to dismiss such trivialities as the passing of a couple of hundred years.

The meeting of the Charstock Residents' Association took place the following evening. The Thorntons attended, in the end, along with Jane's parents. Grandpa came down to baby-sit for the Harveys, and Tim joined him over there. Rather fortunately, neither of Jane's small brothers required attention of any kind, since Grandpa's recipe for the quieting of babies was a good swig of sherry or anything else of that kind that might come to hand. "Always does the trick," he said. "Used it on your mother once or twice. When your grandmother wasn't there, of course." Mrs Thornton, overhearing, was most indignant.

It seemed that the meeting had gone off well, with everybody united in complaints against the council and the development company. A long list of things to be investigated had been drawn up, ranging from the curious behaviour of television sets and washing-machines to the appearance of the brick walls, and an Action Committee had been formed to get something done about it. Mrs Thornton and Mr Harvey were both on the Action Committee and were still huffing and puffing enthusiastically when they got back. Grandpa and the children listened with interest and, in Grandpa's case, a certain amusement.

"Reckon that'll sort it out, do you? Chivvying the council and those building people."

"Well, of course. There's been negligence, shocking negligence. The ground can't ever have been cleared properly or there wouldn't be all these walls cropping up everywhere. And the electricity supply's faulty. The council ought to be looking into it, too, instead of standing by and doing nothing. What do we pay rates for?"

"The site was left in a disgraceful state," Mr Harvey chipped in. "Impossible to get the gardens going."

"Ah," said Grandpa. "How's that box hedge of yours coming along?"

Mr Harvey replied rather shortly that he had had it out and replaced it with cauliflowers.

Grandpa sniffed. "Well, you must suit yourselves. To my mind, you're up against a bit more than Great Maxton District Council and a building company."

"What on earth do you mean, Dad?" said Mrs Thornton irritably.

But Grandpa refused to be drawn further. He merely observed that it never paid to jump to the most obvious conclusion. Thinking along a beaten track didn't get you anywhere; you wanted to look at things in more than one dimension. "The world's a strange place," said Grandpa obscurely. "You ought to take it on its own terms, not on yours."

Mrs Thornton, bidding good-night to the Harveys, murmured that Dad was getting a bit quirky in his old age, you needed to take most of what he said with a pinch of salt. The Harveys nodded understandingly.

The following morning two strange men were seen touring the estate. They were armed with maps, which they frequently consulted, and surveying instruments. They took measurements all over the place and stood about squinting along the roads, peering over garden walls and talking to each other in low voices. They seemed unwilling to do much talking to Charstock inhabitants, though they did admit, upon enquiry, to being from the council. They were just going to check up on one or two things, they said, just have a look at these old walls people seemed a bit worried about, no problem really, they were sure, soon have it sorted out. Charstock watched, with suspicion and a little hostility, from behind its front-room windows.

Jane and Tim also watched. They did more than watch: they trailed behind the council men, and stood around as they measured and consulted. They had nothing in particular to do, it was as good a way to spend the morning as any, and they rather fancied a go at those curious instruments through which the men squinted, not that it seemed a serious possibility. Also, they thought the maps looked interesting. After a while, they closed in until they were only a yard or so away; children are often curiously invisible to grown-ups, as if they were a harmless part of the landscape, like lamp-posts or telephone kiosks. Unless the child in question does something foolish like making a loud noise or otherwise becoming a nuisance, this invisibility can often go on for quite a long time. In this instance, the two men evidently became so used to the presence of Jane and Tim that at one point one of them turned to Jane and held out the end of a tape.

"Here—be a good girl and keep a hold of that for me."

"OK," said Jane.

Another section of road was measured. The men unrolled their map again and pored over it. One of them said, "I reckon the back part of the house was just about here, with the wings to right and left, which no doubt accounts for these remains of walls."

"Charstock House?" said Tim.

"That's right, young man. What do you know about it, then?"

"Nothing much. Just we saw a picture of it the other day."

They were standing in Gianetti Avenue, nearly opposite their own houses.

"It was enormous," Tim continued.

"I don't doubt it."

"The kitchen," said Tim thoughtfully, "must have been just about where my house is."

He reflected upon the smell of roast venison. Of fruit cake cooking. Of mulled wine.

"Very likely," said the man from the council without interest. He unfolded the map again and the two of them leaned over it, talking about drainage and water tables. The children leaned, too. Jane placed a grubby finger on Hammond Drive at a point where someone had written, in neat black ink lettering, SITE OF SHOPPING CENTRE. "That's where it had its lake, this Charstock Park place."

"Now then, young lady," said the council man with an edge of irritation to his voice. "No fingers on my map, if you don't mind."

Jane gave him a withering look. "I was only telling you. I thought you might be interested."

"It's on this old map, as it happens," said the council man, unfurling another sheet of paper. "I pointed it out to you the other day, didn't I, Jim? Of course it was all drained, way back in the last century. And there's the house and the roads through the park and so forth."

"It says 'Charstock Village' there," said Tim. "In funny letters. Right in front of the house."

"That just means where Charstock village once was," said the council man. "In medieval times. It was all swept away when the park was laid out. They couldn't have the view cluttered up with an untidy thing like a village."

The other man began stowing away maps and instruments. "Bit high-handed. You could get away with that kind of thing in those days. Time we were on our way, we've got that other job over in Witney."

The children mentioned this incident to Grandpa the following morning, standing with him in his garden looking down towards Charstock. The houses stood bright and boxy in their neat rows, each with its square of garden fore and aft, their windows snapping in the sunshine. To each side and beyond, green fields striped with the darker green of hedges rolled away into the distance.

"Fancy that," said Grandpa. "Cleared out the old village, did they? That would have been this Samuel Stokes fellow. Got in the way of his plans. Mind, I sympathise, up to a point, as a gardener myself. If you're thinking on a big scale you can't let a trifle like a few houses get in your way." He surveyed his own garden with complacency. "I had to be a bit ruthless myself—dug up the old borders here for my vegetable beds, got rid of the fishpond and the odd path."

"Someone's smoking a pipe," said Jane. "Practically in my face. Ugh!" She sneezed violently.

Grandpa put his spade down and sniffed. "Now you come to mention it, I thought I could smell something myself. How about going inside for some elevenses? I'm feeling a bit peckish."

One thing led to another and in the end the elevenses turned into a full-scale meal, since Jane and Grandpa had a sudden inspiration about experimenting with various hitherto unknown versions of Welsh rarebit. And the upshot of that, of course, was that the children were too full to eat their dinner when they went home and made the mothers suspicious and somewhat angry. Jane and

Grandpa had struck up a very rewarding relationship; they were both people of an inventive turn of mind and an inclination to explore.

That evening Mr and Mrs Thornton went to the cinema. Grandpa came down to keep Tim company and presently Jane joined them—both her baby brothers were screaming at once and she said she couldn't stand the racket.

They watched a comedy show on the telly and then switched over to the news. There was to be a strike of something or other, and a million pounds had been paid for a football player. "I wouldn't have given you tuppence for him, personally," said Grandpa. "The fellow's cross-eyed, to my mind. And big-headed too." The television set gave a sudden crackle, as though in agreement, and the picture juddered and dissolved into a confusion of squiggles. When it resolved itself the newsreader—or at least his top half since that was all you could see—was murky and his features no longer to be made out. "I thought this thing was meant to be one of these coloured affairs," said Grandpa.

Tim gave it a bang. "It is. I don't know why it's gone black and white suddenly." He tried to adjust it. The sound had now gone.

"I can smell that smoke again," said Jane.

". . . and I shall remove the houses as I have before," said the newsreader. "I cannot tolerate such an intrusion on my landscape." His voice was much deeper all of a sudden, rather indistinct and with a curious accent, a countryish accent and yet unfamiliar. Something jutted from his mouth: a long-stemmed pipe?

"Eh?" said Grandpa. "What's the fellow on about now?"

Tim stared at the screen. Something was not right, not right at all. The newsreader seemed to have a kind of hat on, you could just see the outline. No, not a hat. A wig. Tied at the back with a ribbon.

"I spit in their faces!" said the television. "They shall see what I can do, that have the impertinence to meddle with my great scheme." The screen went blank and at the same moment the whole room shuddered slightly. The ceiling lamp swung from side to side, Grandpa's coffee cup danced in its saucer.

"Eh!" exclaimed Grandpa. "Now what's going on?"

"I should think it's an earthquake," said Jane. "Just a small one."

Grandpa poured the slopped coffee back into his cup. "You could be right. Unusual, all the same."

The newsreader came back onto the screen, in full colour and of perfectly normal appearance. ". . . in Zimbabwe, where the Foreign Secretary arrived yesterday. And now over to Bob Dyson for the weather forecast."

At this point the phone rang; Mrs Harvey was saying that Jane was to come home to bed. Jane, returning from the hall, said, "I asked if they had the earthquake. They didn't."

"Interesting," said Grandpa. "Very local indeed, in that case."

Jane sat down on the sofa and began to put on her shoes. "The man reading the news turned into that gardener person out of the picture. Samuel whatsit." Her voice was perfectly matter-of-fact. She tied the laces and got up.

"Ah," said Grandpa thoughtfully. "That's rather what I was reckoning myself."

Tim wanted to protest. He wanted to say that people out of pictures painted two hundred years ago do not suddenly appear on a television screen, talking in a curious accent and then vanishing.

"And then," Jane continued, "he made there be an earthquake or something."

"Bit of an assertive fellow," said Grandpa. "Not to say aggressive. Hmm."

There is some perfectly simple explanation, Tim thought. There is something sensible and ordinary, if only one could think of it.

The front door banged. "There's Mary and Ted," said Grandpa. "I'll be off now too, I think. Got all the leeks to plant out tomorrow. I'll be seeing you, then."

Good-nights were said. Mrs Thornton made more coffee and settled down on the sofa. Tim was told to go to bed. Mr Thornton opened the newspaper. "Anyone ring up?" enquired Mrs Thornton. "Anything happen?"

"Not much," said Tim. "We had a small earthquake."

"Ha ha," said his mother.

"And I think the telly's haunted."

"Yes, dear. And there are fairies at the bottom of the garden, no doubt. Up to bed, I said."

"Was it a good film?"

"Smashing," said Mrs Thornton, putting her feet up. "It was about this couple that gets involved with visitors from outer space. Greenish people with kind of lamp things on their heads and funny eyes. But quite well meaning. They want to take over the world for its own good, and this couple is held hostage."

Tim paused at the door. The television was blank and silent. It seemed to him that there lingered, still, the faintest whiff of a rather pungent pipe tobacco. He looked at his mother. "Personally, I don't believe in that sort of thing."

"Neither do I," said Mr Thornton, turning to the sports page. "It was all extremely far-fetched. Your mother loved every moment of it."

Mrs Thornton yawned. "No need to be sarcastic. It was very well acted. Besides, it was only a story. *Bed,* Tim."

Tim went up. He did some fairly sketchy washing and teeth-cleaning and got into bed. He lay there thinking of the way in which the house had suddenly quivered; it had been a most disagreeable sensation. He hoped it would not happen again. There had been something uncomfortable, also—threatening indeed—about that strange and murky figure on the television screen. Of course, it couldn't *really* be . . .

He fell asleep.

CHAPTER 5

"No way," said the man, staring upwards, "am I going up that scaffolding again. I'm telling you, it shook."

He was one of the men working on the last few uncompleted houses. He stood with his mate, contemplating the site on which they were working, the structure of a house outlined in bricks, steel bars and scaffolding. Jane and Tim, engaged in an aimless tour of the estate in search of diversion, contemplated also.

"Can't have done," said the other man. "I checked those rivets myself. Look, firm as anything. . . ." He placed a hand on one of the uprights of the scaffolding, shook it hard and at the same time climbed upon the lowest horizontal bar.

"Watch it!" exclaimed the first man.

Everything seemed to shudder. The builders' man leaped backwards from the scaffolding and as he did so the steel bars began to lurch and tip. There was a frightful clattering of metal upon brick upon metal. The scaffolding disintegrated into a jumbled heap, bringing with it much of the wall against which it had been erected. A cloud of dust arose. The two men turned upon each other.

"I tell you that scaffolding was double-checked last night."

"Must've been a faulty rivet."

The children, fascinated, had crept closer. Jane said, "Actually it was a sort of earthquake. We're getting them quite often."

"Here, you keep away from that, you two. It's not safe. Go on, clear off now. I'll give you earthquakes!"

Jane shrugged. "I just thought I'd tell you."

They moved off. Behind them, the men continued to argue. The foreman came running up, with others. They stood staring while the pile of rubble continued to smoke dust into the summer morning. Jane said, "That was clever of him."

Tim looked around at the houses, both built and unbuilt, at prams and cars and the milkman's float coming down the hill from Great Maxton. At television aerials and bicycles and dustbins and all the other ordinary unsurprising fixtures of this unremarkable Tuesday morning. He said, "Do you honestly think this bloke is doing all this? Samuel Stokes?"

"Yes. So does your grandpa."

"Those men nearly got hurt."

"Yes."

"If he did that to a house with people in it, there would be an accident."

"Yes," said Jane calmly. "So we've got to stop him doing it, that's what."

You had to hand it to Jane, she didn't mess about; she always went straight to the point.

"How?" said Tim, doing the same.

"I haven't worked that out yet. I shall do."

They walked on in silence. "We could tell people," said Tim. "My mum and dad. Your mum and dad."

"If you told your mum and dad there's this kind of gardener person who's been dead for hundreds of years and he's making greenhouses turn into Greek temples and walls grow and getting into the telly and he may knock our houses down, what would they say?"

There was a pause. "Yes," said Tim. "I see what you mean." After a moment he added, "But Grandpa believes it."

"Your grandpa isn't like ordinary grown-ups."

They turned the corner into Hammond Drive. A knot of people was standing outside the front garden of the nearest house. A woman was crying, with a note of hysteria in her voice. "Look at it! Just look at it—right where I bedded out the African marigolds yesterday."

"It's another of those walls," said someone else. "If you ask me, they want to get the press onto it. There should be an Enquiry. It's a scandal. Covering it up, that's what they're trying to do."

Other voices broke in, to comment and advise. The wall, in the meantime, a line of pinkish bricks just ruffling the surface of a flower-bed in the manner of a breakwater at high tide, sat innocently in the sunshine.

There was a smell of tobacco smoke.

Jane said, "I think we ought to go and see your grandpa."

They sat on Grandpa's garden seat and reviewed recent events.

"What we've got here," said Grandpa, "Is a situation that's not reasonable. It's a situation involving things that don't happen. That oughtn't to happen. People are addicted to reason. People like Ted and Mary. Very sensible too. If you went round expecting the unreasonable, you'd be in a fine pickle. Most of the time. But just occasionally you've got to think flexibly, and that's what folk find it difficult to do. Most folk."

Tim agreed. "They're all busy blaming the council and the builders, when in fact . . ."

"When in fact what they ought to be asking themselves is, what sparked it off in the first place, and what's to be done to put it right."

"What sparked it off," said Jane, "is building the estate here at all. It's woken up this Samuel Stokes person and he's putting back what was here before."

Grandpa stared thoughtfully down at Charstock. "I've not a lot of time for the supernatural, as it happens. I've never reckoned much on it. Table-tapping and things that go bump in the night and so forth. Most tales of that kind don't bear much examination. Load of old codswallop, for the most part, when you look at 'em closely. This is a bit different."

"It's as though," said Tim, "the whole place was the ghost. Only it's coming out real."

"Because of him," continued Jane. "Samuel thingummy. Because of what he's feeling."

"Exactly," said Grandpa. "So the problem is his feelings. Very delicate things, feelings. Quite capable of running on for a couple of hundred years. It doesn't surprise me in the least."

Down in Charstock a builder's lorry crawled like a toy between the matchbox constructions of the new houses; washing flapped on a line; a bonfire smoked.

Grandpa got to his feet. "Slow and steady is how to tackle this one, by my reckoning. Cautious. One false move and you could trigger off a landslide. Perhaps not the most tactful word, under the circumstances."

The children returned home by way of the building site, to see what was going on. The collapsed scaffolding had been moved to one side and people were in the process of taking down the surviving bits of the wall to which it had been fixed. Two men in dark suits, holding clipboards, were in consultation. There was an atmosphere of crisis and a sense of strong words having been recently flung around.

Jane was silent. She had dismissed the interesting matter of what was or was not going on in Charstock for the moment and was deep in Part Nine of a long narrative about the discovery of the hitherto unknown East Pole in which she was the explorer involved and also the leader of his intrepid husky dogs. At this moment she had both fallen into a crevasse (as the explorer) and was busy pulling herself out (as the dog), which was a tricky process and required concentration.

Tim was also silent, for different reasons. He was wondering what would happen if things got even more out of hand than they appeared to be at the moment. He felt as though he were caught up in a process that ought to be a dream and yet wasn't. In dreams anything can happen and most things do; in real life nobody is able to fly downstairs, we seldom behave outlandishly and one thing follows predictably—or fairly predictably—upon another. But here was a perfectly ordinary housing estate where preposterous things were taking place in which only three people believed: two of them children and one of them an elderly man generally regarded as a little eccentric.

That evening, he watched the television intently, wondering if Samuel Stokes would choose to manifest himself. Nothing happened, at least nothing more significant than the occasional crackle or flicker. It seemed as though he were able to choose his time. But why, in that case, one time rather than another? Could it be that it was a question of who was watching? It occurred to Tim that on both of the occasions when Samuel Stokes had appeared, or almost appeared, Grandpa had been present.

He put this point to Grandpa the next day, when he was helping him shovel compost onto his vegetable patch. Grandpa leaned on his spade and considered. "You know, you may have a point. One gardener tends to recognise another. Can't explain it, it's like dogs knowing their own kind, that sort of thing. Could well operate with a fellow like that."

"If he's got strong feelings," said Tim.

"Quite. And now you come to mention it, there's been one or two things a bit funny up here." Grandpa surveyed his own prosperous patch. "I've had a sense someone might have been interfering, as it were. I even suspected old Harry Bragg next door. He's been dead envious of my hollyhocks for years, not that he'd ever admit it."

"Funny in what way?"

"Hard to put a finger on it. I thought someone might have been messing about with my espalier apple, doing a bit of extra pruning. Then just yesterday it seemed to me my last sowing of lettuce seed was coming up out of alignment. Could well be that this fellow's taking an interest. Fair enough, I always like a chat with another gardener, but I don't reckon with interference. Well, we'll have to see."

That evening there was a further meeting of the Charstock Residents' Association Action Committee, of which Tim's mother and Jane's father were members. They returned to report an interesting amount of annoyance on the part of everyone and a determination on action.

"What action?" asked Jane.

It was to be demanded that the council show the estate residents the results of this survey they had made of the appearing walls. The residents would also demand from Stagg's that electricity experts be called in to find out what was causing all the interference with the television sets.

And sanitary inspectors must investigate the reason for the curious smells. "Apparently the Spenders' house is reeking of pickled onions. It's disgraceful."

Charstock had got up a good head of steam; people were fairly crackling with indignation. Stagg & Co., anxious to appear soothing, perhaps, responded satisfactorily and within a few days small bands of businesslike men with instruments and notebooks appeared. One of them called at the Thorntons' house.

"About the electricity. Just doing a check."

Mrs Thornton gave him a conducted tour of the offending television, washing-machine and a toaster which had recently taken to giving out small explosions and showers of sparks. The man switched things on and off and investigated wiring and plugs.

"Can't find anything wrong. All quite regular. Same thing next door. Are you sure you . . . ?"

"I am not," said Mrs Thornton coldly, "given to imagining things. Nor is my next-door neighbour. We are not children."

Tim, overhearing, was about to launch into a violent protest. It had struck him before as unfair that while it is considered in bad taste and is in some respects illegal to imply that women are inferior, all sorts of rude things can be and indeed are said about children. However, he restrained himself; the atmosphere was explosive enough as it was. The electricity inspector and Mrs Thornton parted on extremely bad terms.

This visitor was followed a day or two later by a second man, who crawled around examining the drains. He, too, pronounced everything normal, even though at the time there was a distinct whiff of something very spicy in parts of the Thornton kitchen, to which he seemed impervious. Tim was of the opinion that he actually couldn't smell it.

Other men came and did various kinds of measuring and probing in the gardens of the estate. They were impressed by the Spenders' greenhouse, which had weathered a little and now looked rather more settled. Mr Spender was growing a vigorous creeper up it and Mrs Spender had furnished it with flowery garden chairs and a table. She sometimes sat there knitting and looking remarkably out of place.

"Very nice little job," said the surveyor. "I wouldn't mind one of those myself. Classy. Cost a bit, I don't doubt."

"It turned into this," said Tim, "in the middle of the night. From a perfectly ordinary wooden thing."

The man smiled indulgently. "I must say, you're a fanciful lot around here. It seems to be some kind of epidemic."

The children eyed him coldly.

"There's this lady round the corner insists an ornamental fountain appeared from nowhere beside her washing-line. Says it *grew*. I said, 'Look my dear, you must've ordered it from the garden centre and then forgot about it.' She's not young. You can get a bit vague at that age."

"What about all these walls?" said Tim.

"These walls, son, are neither here nor there. At least, they are here, in a sense, fair enough, but they're not in that people are making far too much of 'em. Residual debris, that's all. Always crops up where there's been earlier building."

"We keep getting these earthquakes," said Jane. "Quite small ones, but earthquakes." She looked stonily at the man, whose eye fell on her heavily-plastered and still faintly-bloodstained elbow, the result of a tangle with some barbed wire that she claimed had attacked her. He looked away quickly.

"Subsidence. Nothing to worry about." Stagg's man

looked down at Jane again, with a visible effort, and patted her on the head, a dubious move since Jane was not the kind of child who invites pats on the head. She shied sideways and glared at him through cracked and grubby spectacles. "Yes, well," said the man with rather less confidence. "Cheerio, then, kiddies, I'll be getting along."

"He's silly," said Jane with contempt when he had gone.

"He doesn't," said Tim, "know how to think flexibly."

They reported these events to Grandpa who listened with interest and remarked that things seemed to be hotting up nicely. It struck Tim that he was beginning to regard the situation with a certain relish. It was late afternoon and Grandpa had dropped in for a cup of tea, which he was drinking in the Thorntons' sitting room. Mrs Thornton was through in the kitchen, and Jane and Tim were trying to make up their minds whether to stay in or go out and quarrelling about it in a half-hearted way. They became aware, all three of them at once, of a most acute and compelling smell of tobacco smoke.

"Aha!" said Grandpa. "Our friend."

Tim decided to try an experiment. He got up and switched on the television. The screen burst into sound and activity, something unexceptional enough about wildlife. Zebras cantered from right to left; the room was filled with jungly noises. "Oh, not *that,*" said Jane. "It's boring. Let's . . ."

The zebras vanished. The set fizzed and crackled for a moment and there appeared the indistinct but now unmistakable outline of a bewigged figure. He seemed to be speaking.

"Can't hear," said Grandpa. "Turn him up a bit." But before anyone could move the words became audible.

". . . for my patience is about to be exhausted. I tell you if you do not act swiftly on my behalf I shall be obliged to take matters into my own hands. And that will bode ill for you all."

It was as though the temperature in the room had dropped by several degrees. Chill stole up Tim's spine; he felt Jane, sitting close up beside him, shudder. They sat absolutely still.

Grandpa cleared his throat. "Absolutely," he said. "Quite so. Every sympathy and all that. But what exactly . . . ?"

"It is a poor kind of garden you have yourself," said the figure, in a rather different tone. "But ingenious of its kind. The apple tree should be harder pruned and you grow a very vulgar kind of flower. A greater elegance could be achieved by the introduction of a more flowing line. The curve and the circle should be employed. . . ."

"You don't plant lettuces in circles," interrupted Grandpa with indignation. "I'd look a right charlie. Besides . . ."

"Enough!" snapped the television. "Who are you to question the wisdom of Samuel Stokes? And now pay attention. I am offended and affronted by this place, by these houses with their strange appurtenances and above all by the mean and shabby nature of their gardens. And all this at the situation of my greatest achievement! I will not have it!"

"Hmm," said Grandpa. "That's all very well. You've got a point, granted. We can see your side of it. But people live here."

"They are an inferior kind of person," snarled Samuel Stokes. "They are persons of no account and must be disposed of."

The kitchen door opened. Mrs Thornton could be heard moving about in the hall. The figure on the television screen began to fade. Its voice became more distant. "See to it! I will have no dealings with the peasantry. Be warned of what I may do!"

The screen blazed into colour and a fine display of flamingoes on some African lake. Mrs Thornton came in. "More tea, Dad? I'm just popping to the shop for a minute. Gracious!"

The table rocked slowly to and fro, overturning Grandpa's cup. The sofa rolled forward by several inches. The carpet, quite distinctly, rippled. Outside, blackbirds rushed about the garden shrieking.

When things returned to normal, two seconds later, there was a crack down the plaster of one wall and a fine fretwork of lines on the ceiling. "That does it!" said Mrs Thornton grimly. "Subsidence or no subsidence, we're not going on like this. There'll have to be an emergency meeting."

Grandpa and the children were silent. They looked at the cracks, at the spilled tea, and at each other.

CHAPTER 6

The emergency meeting, taking place two days later, revealed the fact that a number of other houses had also experienced what were now being referred to as 'tremors.' Someone had a crack big enough to get a finger into right down the kitchen wall. Tiles had slid from roofs; mirrors had fallen and been shattered. The theory was being put forward that the estate had perhaps been built upon the site of some abandoned mine, whose workings were caving in beneath it. Others preferred to attack the quality of the building work and the effect of the contractors' heavy lorries, still passing and re-passing as the final houses were completed. An angry letter was sent to Stagg's demanding an immediate inspection by experts.

The company, turning nasty, replied that this was quite unnecessary, that the minor instances of damage reported were due to 'settlement' and would be repaired free of charge.

The residents of Charstock, getting even nastier, retorted that if they didn't get what they wanted they would hire clever lawyers and cause as much trouble as possible. Furthermore, they would invite newspaper reporters and men from the BBC to visit the estate and be told how suspiciously the company was behaving.

The company, backing down, said it would think about it.

The residents replied belligerently that it had better think quick.

In the meantime, Grandpa and the children considered their personal strategy. It was a problem; indeed, it was several problems. To begin with, Samuel Stokes's instructions, though explicit, were also impossible to obey. He had told them to get the estate removed; that was quite out of the question. Since it was unthinkable that they would ever convince anyone of what—or who—was at the root of the trouble, there was no possible way, even if they wished to do so, of satisfying him.

"Besides," said Grandpa. "I don't care for his attitude. High-handed. Very high-handed indeed. Peasantry! Persons of no account! That sort of talk was all very well in his time but it don't do these days. Come to think of it I'm not sure it did then. But you can't get away with this sort of thing any more, that's for sure."

Nevertheless, Tim was glad to see that Grandpa was no longer enjoying the situation quite so much. "We're up against something," he said. "No doubt about that. I don't like his tone. Aggressive. Distinctly aggressive. And I didn't care for those remarks about my garden. Huh!"

The weather continued fine and dry. Given which, it seemed curious that in part of the estate, the area around the shopping centre, the ground remained so wet underfoot. Everyone remarked on it. You had to splash through large puddles to reach the supermarket and the surface of the unmade-up roads nearby were churned into a muddy quagmire. There were complaints. A letter was written about that, too.

Mr Harvey's double row of small cauliflower plants suddenly wilted and died, despite having been most exquisitely cared for. Two days later young but vigorous shoots of a box hedge reappeared, more extensive this time and spreading itself in a geometrical pattern of circles and lozenges over much of the garden.

Mrs Spender, in a state of excitement that bordered on tears, claimed that several times, at night, she had distinctly heard sounds of revelry coming from her greenhouse. "People get in there," she wept, "and carry on like nobody's business. Drinking and singing and I don't know what. It's disgusting. Not a nice sort of person, not people like us." Since she was known to have hysterical tendencies, nobody paid too much attention.

The smells became more and more pungent. Grandpa, who had become something of an expert, wandered round sniffing and defining. "Guinea fowl today. Guinea fowl with what I'd reckon to be a Madeira-based sauce. Pheasant yesterday, and some kind of a spicy pudding. Not something I'm familiar with. Interesting."

In the meantime, there had been some odd occurrences in Grandpa's garden, which had caused him considerable annoyance. His hollyhocks had been severely affected by an unusual blight and his lettuce seedlings continued to come up in circles. "It's that fellow," said Grandpa. "No doubt about it. Interfering so-and-so." On one occasion, he told the children, he had been pottering around his tomatoes when he had become curiously aware of some kind of presence in the middle of the path, a presence that was both bulky and insubstantial. There seemed to be someone, or something, standing there, a whitish shape. "First of all you could just feel it, as it were, and then you began to see it. A bit vague at first, but then it got firmer, and blow me down if it wasn't one of those classical statues. Some sort of nymph affair on a pedestal."

"I s'pose he was trying to give it to you," said Jane

thoughtfully. "He was trying to make your garden a bit more posh."

"I daresay. But I thought, oh no you don't, I'll make my own arrangements, thank you very much. I don't want a lass without any clothes on stood there every time I'm hoeing the beans."

"What did you do?" asked Tim.

"I walked straight through it. I got the wheelbarrow and pushed it straight through."

"What did it feel like?"

"There was a resistance, I'd say. A slight drag. Nothing much. But it did the trick. When I looked back it was gone. So it goes to show, you can stand up to him."

It was a pity, they agreed, that the residents of Charstock were incapable of taking the same kind of forthright action. "It's a question of meeting him on his own terms," said Grandpa. "There's a limit to what he can do, from that far off, and if you stand up square to him, you're fine. But messing about with letters to the building company and having meetings is playing into his hands."

Samuel Stokes made no more appearances on the television, nor were there any further earthquakes. He seemed, for the moment, to be biding his time.

A further meeting of the Residents' Association was held. The Harveys and the Thorntons attended and reported that it had gone on for hours with everyone getting very angry and excited and people jumping up and down to demand different courses of action. The company had still not given any satisfactory reply to Charstock's demands. It was decided that a delegation was to visit the company's offices at Great Maxton, bearing a request for immediate action signed by everybody in the estate, and carrying placards listing their grievances, so that the state of affairs would become publicly known and the company made to feel ashamed of itself. They would also call at Great Maxton Town Hall and present a copy of the petition to Great Maxton District Council.

"Good-o," said Jane. "A procession. Can we process too?"

"No," replied the mothers, simultaneously.

In the end, however, the children got their way. Jane, in particular, was an expert at wearing down parental resistance. She would stand around looking reproachful and, insofar as a person of her gruesome appearance was capable, pathetic. Eventually people caved in.

Jane's appearance on the morning of the procession was particularly vivid. She wore shorts, which revealed enormous scabs on both knees, the relics of a bicycling incident. She had the remnants of a black eye (an encounter with a door which, she said indignantly, had got itself into a place where it wasn't usually) and a slab of plaster across one cheek. Her father said the Stagg's people would probably take one look and agree to anything just to get her out of sight.

The Charstock delegation, twenty or so strong, walked decorously down Great Maxton High Street, led by Mr Harvey and Mrs Thornton who bore between them a banner which said CHARSTOCK RESIDENTS DEMAND ACTION! and went on to list their various grievances. Tim and Jane thought the banner tame. They had produced an alternative version of their own in red paint with dripping skulls and cross-bones and a portrait of the managing director of Stagg & Co. with a lot of arrows sticking in him. They had not been allowed to bring this and were in consequence feeling put out.

They were met on the doorstep of the Stagg & Co.

offices by the office cat who was sitting in the sunshine engaged in an elaborate grooming operation. It gave them a look of contempt and stalked off. Presently an embarrassed lady emerged and invited them in, saying that Mr Cramp would be delighted to meet them. They crowded into a reception hall, butting into typewriters, rubber plants and enormous ashtrays on stalks. Mr Cramp came in and said how pleased he was to see them, looking the opposite. He read the petition with a fixed smile. Tim and Jane eased themselves to the front and gazed at him to make quite sure he was reading it properly. Mr Cramp caught sight of Jane and flinched, an expression of horror and disbelief crossing his face. He finished reading the petition and said that naturally he personally had the greatest sympathy . . . convinced these little teething troubles could soon be sorted out . . . every co-operation . . . time and patience . . . determined to spare no trouble or expense.

The residents of Charstock listened stonily. The office cat sat on a desk and grinned.

They left. Jane, wading through the furry depths of Stagg & Co.'s expensive carpeting, fell over and crashed into one of the rubber plants, which disintegrated in a shower of soil and leaves.

Great Maxton Town Hall, situated in the middle of the market square, was an imposing building of considerable age, with a flight of steps leading up to a pillared front. The procession was greeted in the entrance hall by a representative of the council, who also made an unconvincing speech about how pleased he was to see them. They were invited into the council chamber to discuss things. There, they stood around awkwardly, glared at from the walls by former distinguished citizens of Great Maxton. The council man talked; various Charstock residents had their say too. Tim and Jane, who had hoped for something altogether more strident, grew bored. Jane, indeed, had imagined a good set-to ending possibly in physical violence and thought this a very feeble affair, with everyone being relatively polite and going on about seeing each other's point of view. That wasn't action. Together, they withdrew from the proceedings and studied the furnishings of the room, in search of something interesting.

There wasn't much, except for an enormous aerial photograph of Great Maxton and its immediate surroundings which was quite fun to examine for its bird's-eye view of things. There was the market square, and the building in which they now stood, and the streets leading off, and the town thinning out and then stopping quite suddenly. And there were the fields that had lain under what was now the Charstock estate, with visible disturbances by way of excavations and a scrawl of tracks and heaps of bricks here and there. The photograph must have been taken a couple of years or so ago, when the building operations started.

The council spokesman had now also turned his attention to this photograph. He was pointing to the fields to the right of Charstock and enthusiastically explaining about something called the Great Maxton Development Plan, Stage Three. Tim and Jane began to listen; there seemed to be possibilities here. Stage Three, apparently, was designed to turn Great Maxton into an even more enticing place than it already was, and to bring more and more people to live and work there, by providing various irresistible attractions. There were to be three football grounds, a cricket pitch, a landscaped park with children's playground and—here the council man drew breath and paused for greater effect—an indoor heated swimming-pool!

"Right next to the estate," said Mr Harvey. "Well, that'll be handy, I'll say that." There were murmurs of approval. The council man beamed upon them, a pin-striped Father Christmas. He patted the petition, which lay upon the shining mahogany council table, and made a further soothing and reassuring speech about the council's concern . . . awareness . . . determination. . . .

Then he ushered them back into the entrance hall and thence once more into the sunshine of Great Maxton's market square.

The delegation made its way home, in a rather quieter frame of mind. It was felt that while Mr Cramp of Stagg & Co. might well be something of a slippery customer and must be kept an eye on, the council had its heart in the right place. This attitude may well have had something to do with the prospect of football pitches, a landscaped park and an indoor, heated swimming-pool right on the doorstep.

The children, also, contemplated this with a certain relish. "I hope it has diving-boards," said Jane. "Twenty foot high ones." Her mother, evidently picturing the association of Jane with diving-boards of any height, shuddered.

They came down into the estate by way of the end which was not yet completed. The remaining house sites, some dozen or so, were rather like a demonstration of how a house grows. At one end of what would eventually be a road was the outline of a house pegged out on the ground with tape. Next door, bricks rose to a foot or so. Further along, walls had reached the top of downstairs windows, and, a little later, an upstairs had been achieved and then the skeleton of a roof. At the far end were two completed houses, both with For Sale signs, one of which was struck through with a sticker saying SOLD. Outside this house there stood a furniture van.

"Ah," said Mrs Thornton with interest. "New people moving in."

Some members of the procession had now dispersed and the banner had been rolled up. The rest, including the Harveys and Thorntons, strolled past the furniture van, casting inquisitive glances at the new arrivals, an unexceptional-looking family who sat on the garden wall having cups of tea from a thermos flask. The removal men were sitting on the tail-board of the van with mugs in their hands. A break was being had, evidently.

It all happened so suddenly that afterwards it was difficult to recall exactly how it was. One moment there was this peaceful scene; the next there was consternation and shouting and people running hither and thither.

The house, the new, shining, empty house with its door hospitably open to its new owners, simply split down the middle. There was a rumble and a grinding noise and what had been the bathroom collapsed into the front porch, the right-hand upstairs bedroom sagged down into the sitting room and the left-hand one lurched uneasily sideways, the bricks jumbling as though shaken up by a giant hand. The chimney snapped off and came rolling down the roof; slates showered into the garden; dust fumed up into the summer sky.

Somebody screamed. Mrs Thornton cried, "Oh, my goodness is there anyone inside?" Several small children started to cry. The next-door dog rushed out barking. Doors opened. People came running down the street.

It was quickly established that the house was, at that

moment, empty. No one was hurt, except for the feelings of the new arrivals' cat, which bolted from its owners' arms and set off posthaste for its old home. The mother of the removed family sat on the wall in a daze, saying over and over again, "If that had happened five minutes earlier . . ." She was persuaded into a neighbour's house for more tea, as an antidote to shock. Indeed, tea began to flow from all sides, as other residents of Charstock gathered with offers of help and sympathy.

There was a distinct smell of smoke, giving rise to suggestions of an explosion of some kind. "Gas," said Mrs Thornton knowledgeably. "That'll be what it was. Or an electrical fault." It was Jane who pointed out that the smell was of tobacco smoke, but nobody paid her any attention.

By the evening, though, the mood of Charstock had turned distinctly nasty. For the rest of the day there was a frenzy of coming and going around the collapsed house: men from Stagg & Co., men from the gas board, men from the council, sightseers. The owners loaded their furniture back into the van and departed, talking threateningly about the action they were going to take against the builders. Rumours spread that the men from the gas board were saying the gas was right as rain and there was no question of an explosion.

In that case, said Charstock darkly, what exactly happened?

A reporter from the county newspaper arrived and took photographs. One of the photographs had Jane and Tim in the foreground, Jane scowling ferociously and with her T-shirt ripped from neck to hem. It appeared in the local paper the following week with the caption 'Charstock children play on unconcerned amid the debris.'

Grandpa did not hear about the event until that evening, when he arrived with a basket of vegetables. By this time there was a considerable fuss going on, with people dropping in to make excited comments and have a say about what they thought ought to be done. It was the general opinion that a crisis point had been reached: the estate was now proven unsafe, and urgent action must be taken. "I won't sleep a wink tonight," wailed Mrs Spender. "I'll be expecting the floor to give way underneath me." A nervous lady down the road had declared her intention of camping in her garden.

The Thorntons' kitchen was so full of people and discussion that Grandpa and the children took their tea through into the sitting room for some peace and quiet. The children related the morning's events, including the confrontations with Mr Cramp and with the spokesman for the council. Grandpa was particularly interested to hear about the Great Maxton Development Plan Stage Three. "Football pitches, eh?" he said. "Landscaped park? Well, well, well." He stared thoughtfully at the blank screen of the television set.

The telephone rang. Mrs Thornton, from the kitchen, called that she was busy and would someone please get that.

Tim answered. There was a deal of crackling and then a distant and unnervingly familiar voice said, "Do you hear me?"

"No," said Tim wildly. "I mean yes. Who do you want to speak to?"

The mouthpiece crackled further and the voice of Samuel Stokes continued. "You have seen now what misfortune I can bring upon this place when I feel so disposed. I had constructed here a landscape which was the admiration of all who came to see it. My walks, my vistas, my lake were the wonder of society. I tell you, I shall bring it back."

"Who is it, dear?" called Mrs Thornton.

Tim put his hand over the mouthpiece. "No one." Under the circumstances, he did not really feel he was telling a lie.

"Pay attention, boy!" snapped Samuel Stokes. "Where is the old man?"

"If you mean Grandpa," said Tim, "he's just having a cup of tea in the sitting room." Daringly, he continued, "You know actually the people you ought to complain to really are the building people and the council man, not us. We just live here, that's all. I'm sure if you . . ." His voice trailed away as he realised he wasn't sure at all.

"Stop your impertinence! I shall decide for myself how best to proceed, not seek advice from a child. Neither will I have dealings with lackeys and tradesmen. Tell the old man . . ."

Mrs Thornton came out of the kitchen. "Tim, I thought you said . . ."

The phone went dead. "Wrong number," said Tim. "Terribly wrong. About as wrong as you can get."

CHAPTER 7

"Versatile fellow, isn't he?" said Grandpa. "Televisions. Telephones. You've got to hand it to him, he's adaptable. Moves with the times."

The telephone incident, though, had been alarming. Worrying, also, was the fact that it had ended unfinished; whatever message it was that Samuel Stokes had wanted delivered to Grandpa, whatever instruction, had been cut short.

Meanwhile, there was quite enough to think about. The stir caused by the collapse of the house continued for several days, with the arrival of surveyors for this and that and interested sightseers from other parts of the estate. Mr Cramp of Stagg & Co. came down himself, several times, looking distinctly less confident than usual, and made a great business of inspecting the site and talking soothingly to people. It was promised that the company's most experienced surveyor—"First-rate fellow, best in the profession"—would visit each house and make a thorough safety inspection.

"Huh!" said Mrs Thornton. "Well, we'll see."

There was a further announcement. A large poster went up in the window of the supermarket, tastefully lettered in old-fashioned looking writing and adorned with drawings of all manner of exotic flowers. Stagg & Company, it declared, were holding a Charstock Garden Competition, in celebration of the completion of the estate in three months' time and to encourage the fine efforts of the residents in laying out their gardens. There would be CASH PRIZES for six runners-up and first, second and third prizes of TWO WEEKS IN HARTLEPOOL, FIVE YEARS' SUPPLY OF TOP-GRADE FERTILISER AND WEED-KILLER and A PAIR OF FIBRE-GLASS EIGHTEENTH-CENTURY STYLE GARDEN URNS.

It looked like a pacifying gesture.

Nevertheless, Charstock was interested. There is nothing like a little neighbourly competition to bring out the worst in people. The prizes were to be given for the most imaginative and attractive garden lay-out. The couple in Lonsdale Road who had penned themselves in behind a solid rank of what appeared to be small dense Christmas trees, were heard to say complacently that they felt they must be certain winners. An elderly bachelor with a patriotic arrangement of the Union Jack in blue and white lobelias and red salvias, clearly thought otherwise. Then there were the people who had installed a garden pool, an elaborately natural affair of grey plastic which had arrived on top of a van complete with goldfish, bulrushes, fountain and concealed lighting. And the garden devoted entirely to families of plastic gnomes peering coyly from the long grass and that in which the flower-beds were bordered with matching pebbles meticulously gathered on some seaside holiday.

People were to be seen taking evening strolls during which they furtively peered over the garden fences of others. The manageress of the supermarket, who enjoyed a joke, said she was taking bets.

Grandpa had grave misgivings about the whole business. "Oh dear, oh dear, oh dear. I don't like this at all. Asking for trouble, this is. If anything's going to put our friend's back up, this will."

"I shouldn't think he'd like these fibre-glass eighteenth-century urns," said Tim. The objects in question were displayed already underneath the poster, presumably as an enticement.

"Quite. Can't blame the chap either. I mean, fair's fair, they thought on a larger scale in those days. He's got his standards. You can't be altogether surprised that he gets a bit hot under the collar."

Tim, who thought this was carrying solidarity between fellow gardeners a bit too far, pointed out that it did not entitle anyone to knock down other people's houses and otherwise interfere with their private lives.

Grandpa, perhaps a mite reluctantly, conceded the point. He was not himself, of course, eligible for the competition, not being a resident of Charstock. "I should think you'd 've won," said Jane. "Easily." Grandpa looked away modestly. "Oh, I don't know about that. Mind," he added after a moment, "there's not many could match my hollyhock bed. But it's production I've always gone in for, more than style. You can keep your fancy lay-outs, as far as I'm concerned."

There was to be a ten-day interval before the judging of the garden competition, to give people time to get themselves properly spruced up. Neither the Thorntons nor the Harveys entered, the Thornton garden being as yet a dispiriting affair of balding turf and a few token plants that Mrs Thornton had shoved in, while Mr Harvey had been more or less defeated by the attentions of his children and the determination of the box hedges, which were now coming up in all directions like an infestation of dandelions. Those households that were entering had been asked to write their names on a list displayed in the supermarket, and were issued placards bearing numbers, which had to be stuck on the front gate. By the date of the judging Charstock had come out in a rash of these, and there was a great deal of snooping around by the competitors to see what they were up against. The manageress of the supermarket was offering five-to-four on the Union Jack arrangement, and three-to-one on the floodlit garden pool, with the rest at ten-to-one.

The judging was to be done by a panel composed of Mr Cramp from Stagg & Co., the man from the council and the manager of the Garden Centre in Great Maxton. On the day, these assembled at the shopping centre, and set forth, armed with clipboards and wearing expressions that were both serious and somewhat aloof; here were people, they seemed to imply, who combined exquisite judgement with absolute fairness. They were followed, at a distance, by a small crowd composed of some of the competitors and a number of children who had nothing better to do, including, of course, Jane and Tim.

It was a still, warm day, rather oppressive. Someone said there'd be thunder before the evening. Mr Cramp, in his office suit, could be seen to be uncomfortably hot. He led his fellow judges off down Gianetti Avenue, running a finger around his shirt-collar from time to time and holding forth upon the attractions of the new estate.

Tim, walking with Jane a few yards behind, also had a sensation at the back of his neck, but in his case it wasn't heat. It was, he realised, the curious tingling sensation that he got when Samuel Stokes was around. He had noticed it before now—twice. Once, on the occasion when the uninhabited house collapsed and again the other day during the telephone incident. And, yes, there was a smell of tobacco smoke. He looked at Jane.

Jane came out of a brief trance in which she had been the leader of an expedition fearlessly hacking its way through a tropical forest teeming with incredibly dangerous snakes. She unwound a cobra from her left leg, knocked off a mamba with one bull's-eye shot from her rifle, and turned to Tim. "What's the matter?"

"I've got a feeling something's going to happen."

"Him?"

Tim nodded.

"Your grandpa said he wouldn't like this garden business," said Jane with a certain satisfaction. She was a person, as Tim was by now well aware, who preferred action at all costs. This was probably why she was always in such a battered state.

Tim, more apprehensive, hoped it wasn't going to be anything too dramatic.

Several gardens were inspected, uneventfully. The judges made notes on their clipboards and consulted in whispers. The attendant crowd strained to hear what was being said. Those who were competing made unfriendly remarks about other people's gardens, rather loudly in some cases.

Eventually, the judges approached the garden in which was the pool with fountain and bulrushes. The owners, who had now—in some haste—also installed a whole line of interestingly mature weeping willows which they were suspected of having dug up somewhere, stepped forwards from the crowd, looking smug. They had been following the judges round the estate, assessing their competitors, and obviously thought they were in a leading position.

"Number Eleven," said Mr Cramp. "Would you like to

lead the way, Mrs er . . . ?" The judges, and as many others as could fit in, filed after the owner through a small gate into the back garden.

There was a startled silence. "Gracious!" said the manager of the garden centre. "That's a very striking entry, I must say. Quite remarkable. Would you call that a grotto, Mrs er . . . ?"

But the owners were speechless, staring, as was everyone else, at the transformation of their garden.

Where there had been a grey plastic garden pool—ambitious, admittedly, but not all that unusual—there was now a rather larger stretch of water over which presided a rocky cavern, plumped down in the middle of the lawn and lusciously covered with various kinds of fern and moss. Water tinkled from some concealed source at the back of the cavern. The walls had, here and there, an elegant encrustation of shells. At either side of the entrance were statues of Grecian-looking ladies, quite naked and striking affected attitudes.

"Well!" said someone. "Wherever did they get those things? That's coming it a bit, in a place like this."

The owner of the garden gave a sudden scream. Out of the grotto stalked a peacock, followed almost immediately by another. A third appeared from a rose-bed, with an ear-splitting squawk. The next-door neighbour, who had been looking over the fence, was shouting angrily that she wasn't putting up with those birds a minute longer.

"It's effective," said Mr Cramp doubtfully. "I'll say that. It's a question of whether birds as a decorative device lies within the regulations. And the statuary, to my taste, is perhaps a bit . . ."

The lady of the house, moaning faintly, had been led indoors by her husband.

Two more peacocks had appeared from a shrubbery and were strolling around, occasionally pausing to screech for a while.

"They've been doing things to it overnight," said the next-door neighbour loudly. "Must've done. It wasn't like that yesterday. They've had contractors in under cover of darkness, that's what."

"Those birds will have cost a bomb," someone else observed. "Not to mention the nymphs or what-have-you."

The day had turned even more oppressive. The overcast sky was leaden and tinged with yellow. Thunder rumbled.

Mr Cramp advanced over the grass and stood in front of the water, staring at the front of the grotto. "Here," he said. "Take a look at this."

Over the entrance to the grotto, it was now seen, was a small stone plaque, somewhat encrusted with lichen and so not instantly noticeable, and on this plaque was an inscription.

" 'Erected in this year of grace 1759,' " read Mr Cramp. " 'Being the crowning achievement of that greatest and most refined of artists, Samuel Stokes.' "

A grey plume of smoke was twisting up from the artfully arranged rocks that crowned the grotto, unnoticed by all except Jane and Tim, who had wriggled their way to the front of the group and were watching, hypnotised. Tim, who had a feeling that things were rapidly coming to a head, simply gazed; Jane was wondering if she would be allowed to take one of the peacocks home and keep it, and reckoning that the chances were slim.

"Hmm," said Mr Cramp. "Well, it's all very fancy, I must say." He turned to look back at the house into which the owners had retreated. The curtains were drawn and there were sounds of excitement and distress.

It started to rain, heavily. Someone produced a large striped umbrella beneath which the judges conferred. After a minute or two, Mr Cramp emerged to announce that they'd better get on with things before the weather turned worse. Since thunder was now rolling all around, this seemed a good idea. They set off at a smart pace for the remaining two gardens on the list, which were inspected rather briefly.

In what had now become a torrential downpour the judges huddled in Mr Cramp's car to make their decision. Eventually Mr Cramp emerged to announce to the few people still left to take an interest—which included Jane and Tim—that the first prize would go to the Union Jack arrangement, the second to the encampment of conifers and the third to a lady who had constructed what appeared to be a small-scale model of the Alps over which crawled a dazzling selection of flowering plants. The judges had reluctantly decided, said Mr Cramp, that the grotto and pool must be disqualified on the grounds that . . . that, er . . . He cleared his throat. . . . That the judges were inclined to the opinion that it exceeded the competition regulations in various ways and birds could not be considered a constructional feature, being of their nature impermanent.

At this point there was a furious roar of thunder and the heavens broke. Mr Cramp scampered back into the car. The crowd, such as it was, backed hastily into the supermarket. The judges departed, spraying puddles to the right and left.

It continued to rain all afternoon. A taxi appeared at the household of the grotto and the owners emerged with suitcases and were driven away. The lady of the house, it was rumoured, had been completely overcome with nerves and demanded to be taken to stay with her sister in Solihull.

The peacocks proved to be quite uncatchable, and spent the rest of the day causing havoc. One of them got onto the roof of the supermarket and paraded up and down screeching hideously. Another went to roost in the turkey oak and had to be brought down by the RSPCA. In the end they were all rounded up and donated to Bristol Zoo where I daresay they still are.

It rained and rained and rained. It rained in spears and in large splashy drops and finally in a continuous blue mist that thickened the air and blotted out the distances so that Charstock appeared to be all alone in a watery grey bowl. Grandpa, who had come down to the Thorntons' for elevenses and was trapped there by the weather, stood at the window and gazed out. He was furious at having missed seeing the grotto, and was waiting for an opportunity to go round and inspect.

"Put his name on it and all, did he? You've got to hand it to him, he goes the whole way, does our friend."

"The peacocks were a brilliant idea," said Jane.

"The peacocks," Grandpa agreed, "were an inspiration."

Tim pointed out that Samuel Stokes must have been extremely annoyed at not having won the competition.

Grandpa studied the grey pall of cloud which appeared now to be almost touching the rooftops. "Annoyed, I reckon, would be putting it mildly."

They were silent for a moment, listening to the drumming rain.

"Do you think," said Tim carefully, "he can control the weather?"

Grandpa shrugged. "I wouldn't have thought so. But there's no knowing what people get up to, up wherever he is. Or down," he added after a moment. "Down seems more likely."

Towards evening the rain at last stopped. The gardens

were now sodden and the roads gleamed with expansive puddles, while the ones that were not yet made up were inches deep in mud. Grandpa splashed off home and the Thorntons settled down for the evening. Mrs Thornton, drawing the curtains, observed that she'd never seen so much water lying around. "There seems to be more, rather than less, since it stopped raining."

"I'll order a rowing-boat, dear," said Mr Thornton cheerfully. "Has anybody seen today's paper?"

CHAPTER 8

When Tim looked out of the window the next morning, he thought at first there was something wrong with the glass. The world, the familiar world of green and brown, of back gardens and a slice of field, had gone bright and light and shining. He rubbed the condensation away and saw that the brightness and lightness were reflections: reflections in water of sky and trees and the backs of houses.

There was water all around. His own garden was under water and the Harveys' and the Spenders'. The Spenders' temple was elegantly mirrored in what had been their lawn. Water lapped the back doorstep and reached away beyond the fence at the end of the garden, delicately ruffled by the wind. The cows in the field had retreated to a piece of rising ground and were standing around in groups of three, looking rather as though someone had arranged them. In the Harveys' garden a solitary moorhen was cruising up and down, occasionally upending to investigate—presumably—the now submerged box hedges.

Tim dressed hastily and came downstairs, where he found his parents staring in disbelief from the front door. Outside, Jane, wearing Wellingtons, was testing the depth of the water on her front path. As they watched, she took an unwary step into a dip, and the water sloshed over the top of her boots. They heard Mrs Harvey bawl furiously out of the kitchen window.

"Right," said Mrs Thornton tartly. "Where's the rowing boat then?"

Gradually, Charstock emerged, incredulous, to consider its situation. One or two people tried to take cars out and abandoned the attempt when they found that the water reached the top of the wheels. Others waded around and went to the aid of those families who had had their downstairs rooms flooded and were hastily moving carpets and furniture upstairs. Fortunately, most people had escaped this fate as by and large the water was not very deep and was kept out of the houses by front and back door steps. There was talk of calling in the army and demanding a supply of sandbags. Some bits of the estate were still high and dry. The shopping centre, though, being at the lowest point, was completely flooded out. Water swirled merrily through the open door of the supermarket and out of it bobbed a tide of cereal packets and crisp bags.

Tim put his boots on and went out to join Jane, who was now soaked from head to foot and busy trying to construct a waterfall at a point where a stream ran between her garage and the Thorntons'. She was too absorbed in this to pay much attention to what Tim was saying.

" 'Course he did it. At least I s'pose he did. Because he was so angry at them being snooty about his grotto thing. Help me get some more stones."

The children of Charstock were entranced. It was not long before some of the older boys discovered that the waters were nicely stocked with fish. Fishing-rods were brought out and by mid-morning the catch amounted to six bream, four tench, one gudgeon, some eels and a creature that Grandpa, who had come wading down from the dry heights of his cottage, considered to be an inland form of mackerel.

Boats appeared. There was not enough depth for the various dinghies and suchlike craft which adorned a few families' garages and back gardens, but some canoes turned out with great success and went careering up and down Gianetti Avenue and McAndrew Way. Races were held and there was excitable talk of a Charstock regatta.

Meanwhile, on the more serious side, a police inspector had arrived and toured the estate with a megaphone, telling people not to worry, an instruction which was received with some coolness. During the afternoon a helicopter buzzed about overhead. Mrs Thornton said drily she supposed it was going to drop bundles of hay, as to snowbound cattle. The manageress of the supermarket put up a somewhat unnecessary notice saying that she was closing indefinitely owing to circumstances beyond her control and left hysterically for Great Maxton.

The sun shone serenely from a sky of palest blue. It shone upon the tranquil waters of Charstock and was reflected back in sparkling rings and ripples which, later, as evening came, turned to a sheet of molten gold. The roofs of Charstock, and its trees and fences, and the hedges of the surrounding fields, arose from this lake of fire so that one had a curious impression of the place having grown up from the waters, rather than the waters having stolen up upon the place. And, as night fell, the first night of the flood, the fire turned to a deep and velvety black, an absolute darkness amid which the houses quietly glimmered, their windows sending long trembling ribbons of light out upon the lake.

For a lake was what, the next day, it was being called. There were news items in several papers, some more strident than others: 'It's lovely weather for ducks at Charstock!' 'Householders splash out!' 'Widespread flooding at midland housing estate; reappearance of eighteenth-century lake.' This last, more sober account, went on to say that local officials, studying the extent of the flooding, considered that recent heavy rain had in some way affected the water table in the area and caused the re-emergence of the old springs which had once been the source of the lake in Charstock Park. One of them was quoted as saying that it was quite remarkable how closely the outline of the present flooding followed the shape of the lake as shown on old plans; "Uncanny, really. It's as though someone had turned a tap on and put the thing back."

The next day the waters were just the same, neither more nor less. They had a comfortably settled look now, washing lazily against doorsteps and lapping round the trunks of trees. Colonies of ducks appeared, some of them rather exotic, and paddled decoratively along what had been the roads of Charstock. Bulrushes and clumps of yellow irises sprang up with amazing rapidity along the fringes of the lake. A kingfisher was seen sitting on the Harveys' television aerial.

The Charstock Residents' Association turned itself into an Emergency Committee and arranged a shopping service whereby those who were able to splashed their way up to Great Maxton and brought back supplies for the rest, which were delivered by punt. The punts, laden with bread, tins, packets of cornflakes and detergent and stacks of frozen chickens were a curious sight, gliding smoothly from front gate to front gate. There was a great deal of goodwill around; Charstock, united in adversity, sank its differences and got down to sorting itself out.

It was rumoured that a massive pumping operation was to be begun.

Grandpa got out his old fishing gear and appeared wearing waders that reached up to his armpits. He set himself up on the Thorntons' garden wall with an impressive array of rods, lines, tins of bait and landing nets. By tea-time he had caught two eels, three perch, a nasty looking creature probably unknown to science, and half a dozen plastic bags, an old sock and one of Jane's lost plimsolls. He arranged his catch on the wall for all to admire and talked happily of fish pie for supper. Tim, who did not fancy the eels, declined his invitation to come up to the cottage for it, as did Jane.

Tim pointed out that people were getting quite used to living in the middle of a lot of water. Sort of settling down to it.

"Very adaptable, people," said Grandpa. "It's remarkable. Did I ever tell you about the time when . . . ?"

Tim watched a party of ducks investigate the front lawn and cruise into the garage. "I'm not sure I'd want to live like this for always."

"I would," said Jane. "It's much better. More interesting. There's more things to do. And we wouldn't be able to go to school."

Tim regarded them both with some irritation. Grandpa was exploring the contents of his bait tin, a glutinous mixture of something quite disgusting, and Jane was trying—and failing—to jump from one gate-post to another without falling in the water. There were times when he felt neither of them were totally responsible people. He stared out over the waters of Charstock, upon which the sun again serenely shone.

Tim thought that never mind old Samuel Stokes and

whoever or whatever he might be, this Charstock Park place must have a great deal of determination of its own. It hadn't existed for nearly two hundred years and yet here it was pushing back against time. Or coming up again through time, whichever way you liked to look at it. You thought of time as being something that just went sternly onwards, whether it was from breakfast to lunch or from this year to next, sweeping all before it, but perhaps in fact there were some things that time couldn't absolutely deal with. Very forceful people, like Samuel Stokes. Or very distinctive places, like this enormous garden or whatever it liked to call itself. Perhaps such presences had the power to keep on bobbing up for ever, in one way or another, rather like odd moments in one's own head: moments of particular excitement or fury or satisfaction. Tim himself carried various such experiences around with him, to be taken out and re-examined from time to time. The panic-stricken moments of being chased by a black dog once when he was very young; the surge of explosive rage against an old enemy at his first school, which had resulted in a famous and prolonged playground battle; rushing about in thick snow; the breathtaking cold slap of a Cornish wave on the first day of last year's summer holiday; the shininess and utter unreality of his first proper bike sitting under the Christmas tree. Like it or not, you were encumbered with such things.

He was interrupted in these thoughts by a flurry of excitement as Grandpa hooked something apparently of great size and resistance which turned out to be a pair of pyjama trousers, presumably fallen from someone's clothesline. Grandpa, disgusted, threw it back and prepared to go home.

Charstock was now at the end of the second day of the flood.

On the morning of the third day lorries and complicated machines appeared on the higher ground of the field beyond the Thorntons' garden. It was said that they were going to pump water, or divert it in some way, into the little river which flowed on the other side of this. A bulldozer was seen to do some excavating; many people came and went.

Throughout that day, and the next, the level of the water remained exactly the same. There was a short rainstorm, but that made no difference either. The lake neither rose nor fell, though the bulrushes and irises spread, water-lilies appeared in the forecourt of the Amoco garage and a heron was seen fishing from the telephone kiosk.

Grandpa made a special trip to a fishing-tackle specialist shop some way away and returned with a large tin heaving dreadfully with yellow maggots. He spent further satisfactory hours on the Thorntons' garden wall and went home to concoct what he said would be the fish soup to end all fish soups.

That evening Charstock featured on the television news. The waters were shown from a helicopter, with the houses squatting stolidly amidst. Tim, peering, thought he could make out Grandpa on the garden wall; on the other hand, it might not have been. It was interesting to be famous all of a sudden.

Most Charstock residents, however, missed seeing this since they were attending a meeting of the Emergency Committee. The meeting was held in the open air on the high ground at the far end of the estate, which was still unflooded. Mr and Mrs Thornton returned to report that this had been an excitable affair, with people all talking at once and demanding action and blaming everyone from the Prime Minister to Mr Cramp of Stagg & Co. It was agreed, noisily, that the pumping operations were having no effect at all. And for the first time people were saying there was something funny about the place. The matter of the walls was brought up again, and the television interference, and the unsatisfactory electricity. Mrs Spender had recounted tearfully and for the umpteenth time the saga of her greenhouse. Another woman, who went in for reading tea-cups and was said to be psychic, declared that processions of people walked through her bedroom every night, talking and laughing. And her dog, who was also extra-sensitive, was driven distracted by phantom cats. Someone else had suffered from what sounded to be a full-scale ball with music and dancing being held apparently underneath their garage.

Several people insisted that they had seen strange animals cropping the grass in their gardens during the early hours of the morning, before the flooding. "Those brown things that come in herds," cried Mrs Spender excitedly. "Like on moors and places."

"Rabbits," suggested a cynical voice.

"No, no. Deer, that's it. I've seen them on the telly. Wildlife, that's what they are."

There was open talk of the vanished Charstock Park and the demolished stately home. Those who had such inclinations mentioned ghosts; those who did not spoke vaguely of static electricity and thought transference. The Archbishop of Canterbury should be brought in, it was suggested; others favoured a team of scientific experts.

The only matter of general agreement was that not enough was being done.

The weather continued warm and dry. Many of the children were now using the lake as a swimming-pool, despite the objections of the mothers who talked darkly about the water being polluted. Truth to tell, it didn't seem particularly polluted; it sparkled and shone and in most places now that the mud had settled you could see the bottom, with waterweeds beginning to grow and an abundance of the mysterious leggy and whiskery forms of life that appear in any pond.

And all the while Samuel Stokes remained silent.

The pumping continued. More men arrived, and more elaborate equipment. Other men waded around the estate, testing the depth of the water with rods and writing things down on charts. The residents made sarcastic comments from their garden gates and front-room windows.

Newspaper reporters descended and went around interviewing people. At first they were received quite amiably; they offered an opportunity to let off steam and make complaints, and of course everyone had a story to tell. But then, on the third or fourth day of the flood, one of the daily papers particularly given to large print and exclamation marks had a piece headlined EERIE DOINGS AT CHARSTOCK in which the residents were represented as an excitable lot, given to exaggeration and fantasy: 'Estate dwellers claim that . . . Mrs B., a fifty-year-old housewife who "hears things," insisted that . . . Fantastic tales of greenhouses that change into Greek temples . . .' After that Charstock clammed up; doors were banged in the faces of the reporters. Returning to their cars, they found blunt messages tucked beneath the windscreen wipers: GO AWAY, KEEP OUT.

The residents of Charstock, in fact, were taking up a somewhat curious attitude. They were closing ranks; their only friends, they felt, were each other; their anger was now directed against the outer world in general, and not just Great Maxton District Council and Stagg & Co. Extraordinary events were having an extraordinary effect. Tim overheard a conversation between a couple of the surveyors' men who were going round testing the depth of the water. They were of the opinion that the people on this estate were a bit of an odd lot. Irritable. Tetchy. Outspoken. Quite a few temperamental types around, too. One of the men referred to the business of the walls, the earth tremors, the electrical faults. "All a lot of palaver," said the other dismissively. "Good deal of fuss about nothing. On the other hand"—he stared down into the water that swirled around his boots—"subsidence and residual debris I can account for, reappearing lakes is another matter. It doesn't make sense, frankly."

Tim repeated this remark to Grandpa, the next time he and Jane were up at the cottage. They stood, all three, at the end of Grandpa's garden looking towards Charstock, where a sheet of white water glittered in the sunshine, with the rows of houses marching down into it, a curious sight to say the least of it.

"Of course it doesn't make sense," said Grandpa with satisfaction. "Silly fellow. Fancy expecting the world to make sense."

Jane studied a mutilated knee. "Some of it does. Like sharp things scratch you and if you fall on something hard it's you that gets hurt, not it."

"That's physics," explained Grandpa. "Science. Science makes sense, up to a point. They've got all those smart johnnies in laboratories seeing to it that it does."

Tim commented that one might have thought a lake to be physics, of a kind. Water.

"It's an element," Grandpa acknowledged. "I'll give you that. But the point is, it's not elements we're up against here, it's feelings. Human feelings. And human feelings have nothing to do with science. So you don't go asking for sense where no sense ought to be expected."

There was, one had to admit, a certain basic truth about this. Tim pondered for a minute or two on the various unsensible human responses one came across. In one's own home, for instance. That very morning his father had fallen over the cat, which was not the cat's fault, and dropped his tea-cup in the process, at which point he had lost his temper and turned on Tim. None of which was sensible, though probably human.

"And it wouldn't do a blind bit of good," Grandpa continued. "Sitting down to explain to this Samuel Stokes chappie, all nice and rational, how he'd better see sense and face up to the fact that he's not around any more nor his works, fancy though they may have been, but that Charstock housing estate darn well is."

In the distance, beyond the estate, the pumping machinery could be seen outlined against the sky, like some exotic new growth of trees.

"And I wouldn't reckon much on their chances, either," Grandpa added.

Tim gazed down at Charstock. The last few weeks, since they had come to live there, had been quite the most peculiar time of his life. Interesting, also; alarming, occasionally. He had a strong feeling that Jane, with her taste for an eventful life at all costs, wouldn't particularly mind if things continued thus, but so far as he was concerned, he felt that he had had about enough. He didn't want to spend the rest of his life living in the middle of a lake.

He said, thoughtfully, "If it's no good explaining things to him straight out, maybe you could trick him somehow."

Grandpa looked doubtful. "You're up against a canny sort of a fellow."

"He's older than us, too," Jane added. "About two hundred years older."

"Being older doesn't necessarily make you cleverer," said Tim.

Grandpa sniffed loudly as an indication that offence had been taken. "I wouldn't be so sure about that."

"What I was thinking," Tim went on hastily, "was that maybe we could kind of get his attention off Charstock. Get him interested in something else."

"He isn't interested in anything except gardening," said Jane.

"Then it would have to be something to do with gardening."

"Such as?"

At this point Tim had to admit himself defeated.

Grandpa, however, said that maybe he was onto something. They'd better all work on it and see what they could come up with.

The children went home, rather silent. Tim was turning over in his mind the question of tricking Samuel Stokes. He tried to turn himself into an arrogant, vain and obsessive person who in fact no longer existed but considered that he did, and to work out how, if you were such a being, you would respond to things. It was a difficult process, to say the least of it. Jane did the same for a minute or two and then gave up in favour of an absorbing personal fantasy in which she was deeply involved, inspired by recent events. In this, she was an intrepid sea-captain in pursuit of a famous and dastardly pirate. The pursuit went on, night and day, around the waters of Charstock, which had been fitted out with fearful storms, hidden reefs on which many a ship had foundered, sea-monsters and much else for the occasion. Jane was, of course, both the sea-captain and the pirate and occasionally a sea-monster into the bargain. Thus engaged, with all cannon blazing and the ship under full canvas, she fought her way down into Charstock.

CHAPTER 9

The estate had now been flooded for a week. It was becoming a way of life. The postman had acquired a punt and was to be seen poling up and down with great speed and dexterity. There was a regular system of deliveries from the Great Maxton shops. Those residents whose houses were in the part that was still high and dry felt quite out of things. Others who had had more to put up with, in the deepest part of the lake near the shopping centre, were living an upstairs life with considerable bravado. One lady was shown on the television news, hanging her washing out on a pole from her bedroom window and hauling up provisions in a basket.

All the while, there was no sign at all from Samuel Stokes. The televisions were less subject to interference than ever before. The mysterious smells died down. There were no manifestations of tobacco smoke. It was as though, in triumph and perhaps in completion of what he had set out to do, he had taken his departure.

Mrs Thornton, looking out of the front-room window over the now familiar watery view, said, "Hello, we've got visitors."

A punt, occupied by four men in dark suits and poled by a chauffeur in a peaked cap, who looked surly at the indignity, was making its way down Gianetti Avenue. Three of the men were strangers; the fourth was Mr Cramp of Stagg & Co., who had not shown his face in Charstock since the flood. Mrs Thornton snorted indignantly. "I don't know how he's got the nerve."

Mr Cramp appeared uneasy. He was doing a lot of talking. His companions gazed impassively around, as though touring a flooded housing estate in a punt were an everyday affair. One of them took notes from time to time on a large pad.

The punt disappeared into McAndrew Way. The postman, following in its wake, delivered an anxious letter from Mr Thornton's mother, who had read of their plight in the papers, and a brochure from a firm manufacturing small garden swimming-pools. Mrs Thornton wondered angrily if this was some kind of a joke and threw it in the waste-paper-basket. Meanwhile the postman, ever a bearer of news, was saying that the visitors were very important people from the Ministry of Something, carrying out an Enquiry.

"Enquiring's not going to get us dried out," said Mrs Thornton. "It's action we want, not blokes in posh suits coming round enquiring."

"Right," agreed the postman, who now regarded himself as an honorary Charstock resident. He added that Stagg & Co. were also being Enquired into, which was why Mr Cramp was looking so agitated. He hinted darkly that Stagg & Co.'s building standards were under suspicion, a suggestion that was warmly taken up by Mrs Thornton. Tim, listening, couldn't help feeling a bit sorry for Mr Cramp who didn't after all know what he was up against. He pointed out, cautiously, that some people thought it was all to do with this park place that used to be where Charstock now stood.

"Oh, I daresay, son," said the postman. "I'm not saying that might not come into it. But an experienced firm of builders should be able to deal with a little thing like that."

There was not much point, Tim decided, in pursuing the matter. Seeing Jane at the gate, he went out to join her. Together, they splashed their way idly down the road to see what, if anything, of interest might be going on.

The events that I am about to relate may well seem shocking to you: improbable, even. Shocking in that people do not normally behave like that and improbable for the same reason. But, as you will have already gathered, we are dealing with exceptional happenings, and whether what came to pass in Charstock over the next half hour was any more strange or unlikely than the transformation of a cedar frame greenhouse, a washing-machine that gave forth the smell of roast venison or brick walls that could grow up overnight, you will have to judge for yourself.

Jane and Tim rounded the corner into Hammond Drive and sighted, in the distance, the puntful of visitors, which had come to a halt and tied up to a lamp-post. Some sort of discussion was going on. But the punt had acquired an attendant convoy of canoes, other punts and various people clad in the now standard Charstock gear of waders or knee-high Wellington boots. Everyone was staring at the visitors not in admiration but with distinct hostility. Tim and Jane, interested, waded nearer.

The visitors conferred. Mr Cramp could be seen to be holding forth. At one point a couple of canoes approached the punt and he waved them back in a domineering fashion. "Kindly keep away. This is not a public discussion!"

"Cheek!" exclaimed a bystander. "It's public all right as far as I'm concerned." There were murmurs of agreement.

"Action!" shouted someone. "That's what we want. Cut the talk and let's see some action!"

The gentlemen from the Ministry, as though mildly bothered by some background noise, a passing aircraft maybe, or intrusive traffic, glanced round and drew closer together over their notepads and files.

The shouting increased. Some of the things said were not very polite. In fact they weren't polite at all. Some remarks were passed about Mr Cramp. It was indicated that he might not be entirely welcome in Charstock.

And then Mr Cramp made the mistake of replying. He stood up in the punt—which rocked alarmingly—and shouted that people in these parts were an over-excitable lot, that was the trouble, and if they'd only have a bit of sense and leave it to . . .

It was impossible to see where the clod of earth came from. Given that there was little earth around at the time that was not covered by water, a window-box or flower-pot seems likely. It landed smack on the notepad of one of the men from the Ministry, showering all of them with dirt.

There was laughter. Another object, which appeared to be a wet dishcloth, landed in the punt with a shouted suggestion that it might be useful for mopping up.

Jane and Tim, who I am sorry to say were not as appalled by these deplorable goings-on as they ought to have been, were now in the forefront, watching expectantly.

The men from the Ministry brushed down their dark suits, no longer looking quite so detached. One of them said something rather sharply to Mr Cramp, who was now shouting and waving his arms around even more. Mr Cramp sat down abruptly and the chauffeur began hastily to pole the punt on along Hammond Drive.

What followed was, I suppose, the victory of Charstock and the ignominious retreat of the authorities, if such you could call them. The ministerial punt made its way back towards the unflooded end of the housing estate where the ministerial car had been left, closely pursued by a raggle-taggle collection of followers, of every age and condition. There were children, enjoying themselves hugely, and there were, I'm afraid, grown-ups also; and whose comments were the loudest it would be hard to say. There were no more missiles thrown—at least Charstock retained some sense of decency—but this was fully made up for by insults and general indications that men from London in dark suits would do well to stay away, and Mr Cramp also and in particular.

At the water's edge the four men scrambled hastily from their punt, piled into the car and departed at high speed. Whether or not the Ministerial Enquiry was ever completed I'm afraid I cannot tell you.

Tim and Jane returned home. Jane, sploshing happily through the deepest bits, said, "That was good."

They reported back to Mrs Thornton, who remarked sternly that people seemed to have been behaving disgracefully and then added less sternly that she wished she'd been there.

News of the event spread rapidly through Charstock and indeed by the afternoon had reached Great Maxton. Grandpa came down to hear what had been going on. He also made token noises of disapproval which turned into requests for more precise descriptions of what exactly had happened. "I suppose you might call that a riot," he remarked. "On a smallish scale, of course. I take it there wasn't any bloodshed?"

"No," said Jane, with a trace of regret.

"Just as well. We'd have had the newspapers down here again."

That evening a further meeting of the Emergency

Committee was held. It took place once again in the open air on the dry ground beyond the estate and on this occasion Jane and Tim managed to attend, unobserved, lurking around behind grown-up backs and under grown-up elbows. It was a noisy and confused affair, and they were interested to note that grown-ups under such circumstances spend most of their time doing exactly what children are told not to do: they interrupt each other, contradict, all talk at once, shout and so on and so forth. Desperate and not very successful attempts were made by Jane's father, as chairman, to keep things under control. Somebody wanted to organise a protest march to 10 Downing Street and somebody else was sure that if they only wrote a letter to the Queen she would soon get something done and another person was anxious to make effigies of the various villains of the piece and parade them around Charstock in a punt.

It was now a matter of some confusion, though, who the villains of the piece actually were. Mr Cramp was still widely mentioned, as were the members of Great Maxton District Council. But the government were now being blamed, and the Russians and the Common Market and insecticides and sonic booms and somebody's mother-in-law who had recently visited Charstock and was well known always to bring trouble.

Everyone, in fact, except the real villain. Which, under the circumstances, was natural enough. Tim, returning home across the field, wondered if Samuel Stokes had been, in some vaporous way, present at the meeting.

"Of course," said Jane, as though developing his thoughts, "he isn't exactly a ghost, is he?"

Whatever a ghost may be, thought Tim. The point about Samuel Stokes seemed to be that he was able to make a whole place behave like a ghost while not, in the accepted sense anyway, actually being one himself. No nonsense about wandering around in white sheets or creaking floorboards or what have you. It was altogether a more advanced business than that. Which, of course, was partly what made it the more inconceivable that anyone would ever believe it if you tried to explain it to them. Straightforward ghost stuff would probably get a more sympathetic hearing. But a whole non-existent landscape reasserting itself . . .

That night a wind got up. Tim, lying in bed, could hear the water outside, slapping gently against the garden fence. It was an interesting noise, like being at the seaside, or on a boat, but it made him think once more that he did not at all want to go on living like this for ever. Unlike Jane and his grandfather who shared a somewhat disorderly approach to life, Tim was a person who liked things to be reasonably normal. Which could not be said of the present situation. Houses are not usually surrounded by water. He lay, reflecting, and outside the water rustled and when at last he fell asleep he dreamed of peacocks and grottoes and disappearing statues and a lake astride which stood a gigantic black-coated figure, whose head was lost in a wreath of swirling cloud that smelled strongly of tobacco smoke.

It became apparent, during the next few days, that accounts of Charstock's truculent mood had reached the members of Great Maxton District Council. The local paper reported a statement by the chairman which went on at some length about how worried they all were over the 'distressing' situation of the new housing estate and what tremendous efforts were being made to do something about it and how sure the council was that everything would work out all right in the end. It ended by saying rather mysteriously that the council would shortly be making an important announcement which would be of special interest to the residents of Charstock.

"Huh!" said Mrs Thornton. "They're going to give us all a free issue of water-skis, I don't doubt."

It was several days before this promise was followed up, and when it was it took the form of a typed circular on pink paper delivered at every Charstock house by the postman, whose round was made even more leisurely than usual by the fact that he could not resist pausing to explain the contents of the circular at every door before the recipients had time to read it.

"It's this Development Plan Stage Three. It's been brought forward. It's to go ahead right away."

Mrs Thornton inspected the circular. She snorted. " 'Dear Ratepayer . . .' I like that! Buttering us up, that's what they're doing."

Tim peered over her shoulder. "Cor! The swimming-pool's going to be ready for next summer! Landscaped park . . . football pitches . . . recreation areas . . . children's playground."

"It's a sweetener," said Mrs Thornton. "That's what."

"You've got a point there," agreed the postman. "Number twenty-two said exactly the same. And The Firs says she'll believe it when she sees it. Cheerio, then."

Mrs. Thornton and Tim studied the circular over the kitchen table. It did indeed give the impression of offering the children a treat if they promised to behave nicely in the meantime. Mrs Thornton snorted again. "Well, we'll see. It's just a lot of blarney, I suspect." She put the notice on the kitchen pin-board saying darkly that she might want to wave that in their faces in the fullness of time.

However, as it turned out within a day or two, she was wrong. Jane and Tim, who were beginning to exhaust the possibilities of water (as Jane said, you can build dams and streams and waterfalls and whatever but what do you do with them when you've got them?) had wandered over to the unflooded fields to the east of the estate. There, to their surprise, they found a scene of considerable activity. Men were pegging tapes out on the ground, and a bulldozer was at work grubbing out a hedge. Others crawled around scooping out soil and generally scarring the landscape. Clearly, something quite ambitious was going on and when the children were able to persuade one of the men to answer their questions they discovered that this was, in fact, Great Maxton Development Plan Stage Three, in all seriousness.

They stood and watched for a bit, having nothing better to do. There was something impressive if disconcerting about this instant and devastating interference with the landscape. Yesterday, a field with cows and hedges and in one corner a small copse; today, a litter of smashed brushwood, a rapidly expanding hole, and grass mangled by bulldozer tracks. Tim was reminded of something. For a while he stared, in a trance, unable to nail down what exactly it was this made him think of. . . . The bulldozers trundled to and fro, brown water began to seep into the bottom of the hole they were scooping, another sapling crashed to the ground.

And then all of a sudden it came to him. That picture in the Ashmolean Museum of Samuel Stokes standing amid the blighted scene that he was transforming into his park.

Samuel Stokes ought to be finding this interesting, if he was around. Quite like old times.

In which case . . .

"I've got an idea," cried Tim.

An hour or so later they were at Grandpa's.

Grandpa studied Tim thoughtfully. "Brains. No two ways about it. Definite indication of brains. I've always said as much to your mother."

Tim looked away modestly. "Do you think it might work?"

"It could. It might indeed. Let's just go over it again. We get in touch with our friend and we mention to him that there's this park being laid out alongside Charstock. Big project. Large-scale. Lot of scope for a professional. And we point out they seem to be in need of direction, as it were. . . ."

"So," interrupted Jane, "that he gets all interested and then he gets the idea and he moves over there and stops messing about with Charstock."

"Precisely," said Grandpa.

They went over the details. There were two problems: one was how to persuade Samuel Stokes to leave Charstock alone entirely and indeed restore it to its original waterless condition; the other, and perhaps larger problem, was how to get in touch with him.

It was a good ten days or so, they realised, since there had been any indication at all of his presence.

"Hmm," said Grandpa. "Tricky. Not just a question of laying your hands on a stamp, or looking up a phone number. Definitely more abstract than that. An abstract sort of a bloke, our friend."

Tim pointed out that Samuel Stokes had, on one occasion, been known to make use of the telephone himself.

"True. Fact is, he likes to make the first move. Keep the initiative. But we can't wait for that. Not this time."

They sat on Grandpa's garden seat, pondering. "Better have a bite to eat," said Grandpa. "It can do wonders for the mental processes." He went indoors and returned presently with a plateful of toasted cheese and onion sandwiches, one of his specialities.

Jane took an appreciative bite. "I wonder if they had this sort of thing in his time."

"No," said Grandpa. "It would have been altogether more fancy. For the nobs, like him."

Tim felt, again, the unfolding of an idea. First it was like a kind of interesting tickle in the head and then there it was, fully developed and ready to serve up.

"Suppose we invited him to a party!"

Grandpa responded with enthusiasm. "A banquet. Good thinking. Push out the boat. Go to town. A proper nosh-up."

"He couldn't exactly join in the eating part," said Jane.

"Fair enough. It would have to be the thought that counted. I daresay he'd take the point."

"And we could eat his share."

"Quite."

"What would we have?" asked Tim.

Grandpa finished his sandwich and sat silent for a moment. "You'd have to go all out and cater for his tastes. Provide the sort of set-up he's used to—was used to."

"Such as?" enquired Jane.

"Let's see now. Eighteenth-century mansion grub? Well, I'm no expert but I reckon the sort of thing we'd have to lay on would be, um, peacock pie, a carp maybe, or roast pike, yes, roast pike would do if we could rustle one up. Syllabubs. Ales of one kind and another"—Grandpa's enthusiasm mounted—"I wonder if I could lay my hands on a guinea fowl? I suppose a swan might be overdoing it and you could get trouble with the Thames Conservancy people. Pigeon, possibly. A hare. That sort of thing."

The children were somewhat aghast. Jane said, "I'm not sure I like peacock pie. Not that I've ever had it."

"No beefburgers?"

'Definitely no beefburgers. D'you want the fellow to think we don't know what's what?"

Tim spotted a further difficulty. "How do we let him know it's happening? That it's specially for him?"

"I think," said Grandpa, "we may have to trust to luck there. We'll have to reckon on him being a bit of a nosey-parker and cottoning on to the fact there's something up. After all he's been pretty quick off the mark up to now."

CHAPTER 10

Grandpa failed to catch a pike but managed several eels and a thing that looked to the children suspiciously like a goldfish but that he said was a carp or as near as made no odds. After some more ambitious talk about swans and peacocks he settled for a couple of pigeons from the butcher in Great Maxton and various frozen chunks from the supermarket labelled CHINESE RABBIT PORTIONS. Half a bottle of sherry went into a lavish creamy mass that he called syllabub. The mere smell of it made Tim feel queer around the legs, but Grandpa had a happy time stirring and tasting.

On the afternoon scheduled for the banquet Grandpa discovered that he couldn't get everything into the oven. He stood in the middle of the kitchen, which was thick with a combination of smells forceful enough to make you gasp, and stared in perplexity at his array of pans and dishes. It was Jane who suggested that they should build a fire in the garden and cook at least the fishy part of the menu on that. "We used to do it on the school camp. Lovely. Everybody got smoky and the food was mostly burnt."

Grandpa seized on the idea with enthusiasm. "Good plan. It takes me back to exercises on Salisbury Plain in the war. Did I ever tell you about the time when . . . ?"

"The Spenders do it in their outdoor bit next door," said Tim. "Only it's called a barbecue and Mrs Spender got it off a special offer in the Sunday paper and it's always going out."

"All you need," said Grandpa, "is a couple of bricks and a lot of puff. Come on."

What followed might, I suppose, have been predicted. It is not difficult for even the most single-minded people to become distracted from a purpose. The process of building the outdoor oven, and finding fuel for it, and getting the fire going, and the cooking on it, became so compelling and so enthralling that all else was forgotten. "Herbs," said Grandpa excitedly, dashing up and down his garden path. "Let's try a spot of . . . Let's see if a smattering of . . . Keep blowing those ashes, keep up a nice steady glow."

The most exotic and heady fumes arose. Grandpa's next-door neighbour peeked over the wall and then retired again hastily, no doubt lest she be invited to join the feast. Grandpa's neighbours were familiar with his cooking binges.

Grandpa had a sudden inspiration about steeping the so-called carp in vinegar and then wrapping it in vine-leaves, a tricky business producing even more outlandish smells.

Jane decided to use the edges of the fire for roasting some potatoes. It occurred to Tim that the potatoes would be improved by a stuffing of peanut butter.

Grandpa decided it might be an idea to mull some wine while they were about it. Further heady fumes arose.

They ran out of fuel. Grandpa, carried away, piled up peasticks and dead leaves. The fire flared up and for a few interesting moments threatened the clothes-line before it subsided once more to a manageable state.

The eel stew, simmering nicely, had a somewhat pallid look so Grandpa started off to find some onion and a carrot. "Adds texture," he said, prodding with a length of bamboo. The fire was now uncomfortably warm at close quarters. The children felt slightly kippered and Jane had black smudges of ash all over her face. None of them gave a thought to Samuel Stokes.

"Oops!" cried Grandpa, dashing into the kitchen in response to some rather lurid smells of burning pigeon. "Smoky in there," he said, returning. "Here, that carp wants turning over."

Since Grandpa's feasts never had paid any attention to generally accepted mealtimes the fact that it was now about half past three in the afternoon was neither here nor there. Truth to tell, the children were not even much interested in the prospect of eating; it was the cooking that was so absorbing. They crouched around the fire, stoking and poking, as though involved in some kind of magical ceremony. The next-door neighbour came out and removed her washing from the line, with remarks about all that smoke. Grandpa and the children were too busy to notice.

There was rather a lot of smoke. Some of it smelt more like tobacco, too, than bonfire, but they did not notice that either. At one point the blue skeins of smoke arising from the garden curled themselves around Grandpa's runner-bean poles in a pattern curiously suggestive of writing, but no one remarked upon this except the next-door neighbour who had had new glasses recently and didn't trust half of what she saw in any case.

"Time to have a taste," said Grandpa cheerfully. "Pop inside and get us some plates and a spoon or two, there's a good lad." They had gone beyond such refinements as table-laying.

Tim went into the kitchen which was if anything even

more smoky than the garden. He collected plates and cutlery and was about to go out again when it struck him that there was a curious noise in the room, as well as much steam, smoke and smell. His eye fell on Grandpa's radio, standing on the dresser and emitting a high-pitched whistling that suggested it was not properly tuned. He put his hand on the knob to turn it off and jumped backwards as though he had been burned.

The voice of Samuel Stokes boomed forth. "Tell the old man there should be nutmeg with the ale. The pigeons are not sufficiently seasoned."

"Yes," said Tim. "Right. OK. Half a mo."

He dashed out into the garden. "Quick! He's come!"

Grandpa put down his bamboo stirrer. "Eh? What's that?"

"Him!"

Jane and Grandpa hurried inside. The radio, though, was now deeply into 'Afternoon Theatre.' Tim twiddled the knobs, a little gingerly, but got only a blast of pop music and then a racing commentary.

"Hmm," said Grandpa. "What wave-length's he on? That's the problem."

"I must have moved it by mistake," said Tim, twiddling frantically. "I can't remember where it was now." There were whistlings and faint howlings and then a violin rushing flamboyantly up and down the scale.

Grandpa peered at the set. "Shouldn't think he'd go much for Radio One. Try Three, that's more his cup of tea. Cultural stuff."

Tim twiddled some more and got someone talking excitedly in a foreign language, against what sounded like a gale at sea.

"What do the numbers mean?" asked Jane.

"Oh, frequencies, wave-bands and that," said Grandpa vaguely. "Technical business."

"Try 1750," suggested Jane. "That's about when he was, isn't it?"

Tim was inclined to protest that that couldn't possibly make sense but Grandpa agreed with enthusiasm. "Good idea. Imaginative. That's an example of not thinking in straight lines. Like he'd do himself, a fellow like that."

Tim turned the knob slowly. The red line on the glass passed through 1700 and 1750 and at about 1754 there was the most appalling crackle that had them all clapping their hands over their ears.

"Onion sauce!" boomed the radio.

"Eh?" said Grandpa.

"Onion sauce, confound you! Where is the onion sauce that should be served with the rabbit pie?"

Grandpa cleared his throat. "Ah. Now there you have me, I'm afraid. Perhaps a spot of Branston pickle . . ."

The radio crackled and popped. Tim nudged his grandfather. "Tell him. Tell him about the other thing."

But Samuel Stokes was off again. "A carp roasted should be stuffed first with marjoram and dill. For pigeons, make a gravy from cider and thicken it with apple. I am sorely displeased that you did so ignore my greeting."

"Greeting?" said Grandpa doubtfully. "Awfully sorry, none of us ever heard. . . . Busy with the fire, you know, and so forth. You said something?"

"It is written yet," snapped the radio, "for those that have eyes to see."

Grandpa and the children stared around the room, and then out of the open door into the garden, where smoke billowed up from the fire and mixed with . . . "Oh, yes," said Jane. "I see. Above the runner beans."

And there indeed, lightly scrawled against the leafy background was a smoky trail of letters. *S* and *A* and *M* and *U* and *E* and . . . Fading now and disintegrating like the outline of an aeroplane's vapour trail.

"Ah," said Grandpa again. "Very neat. Stylish, I call that. Well now . . ."

He cleared his throat and continued, rather formally, "Very pleased to have you with us. Very honoured. Hope you'll make yourself at home. The thing is, you see, my grandson here and Miss er . . ." He looked dubiously at Jane who, smoke-smudged and with holes in both knees of her jeans, did not really look like Miss Anything. ". . . and young Jane, well, we've got a proposition to put to you."

The smell of tobacco smoke was now overpowering. Jane had a fit of coughing.

"Proceed," said the radio, really quite graciously.

Grandpa, encouraged, continued. He talked about Great Maxton Development Plan Stage Three, except that he did not call it that. He explained that there were these people who were laying out a magnificent new park, in which there were to be gardens and ponds and avenues and . . .

"A prospect," interrupted Samuel Stokes. "Where is their prospect? Fountains? A vista?"

"Ah," said Grandpa. "Now I was just getting to that. You see, these fellows . . . Well, they're doing their best I don't doubt but the point is, they're only amateurs, as it were. Whereas . . ."

The radio made some comments which could not be sorted out from background atmospherics.

"Quite," continued Grandpa. "Absolutely. Whereas if an expert—possibly even yourself, say, if by any chance you felt inclined—if an expert were to take a hand, we might get something really outstanding."

"My work here is complete," said Samuel Stokes. "I have already restored my lake, my temple, my grotto, my . . ."

The children looked anxiously at Grandpa. How was he going to cope?

But Grandpa was off again already, as smooth and persuasive as you like.

"And very nice too. A trifle—repetitive, perhaps? Same old thing? Now an entirely new site . . . Back to the drawing-board . . . Might inspire a major work."

There was silence. The radio hissed and whistled. Then the sound cleared and Samuel Stokes was heard again, in tones of complaint. "My grotto above all was a miracle, an object of the most delicate artistry, a . . ." There was a crescendo of crackling. ". . . and the fools and knaves that did . . ."

"A misunderstanding," said Grandpa. "Not worth your attention. Fools and knaves is quite correct. Now . . ."

There was a volley of, apparently, distant machine-gun fire from within the radio.

"Of course," continued Grandpa in a more offhand tone. "You'd need to clear away the old park again. Drain the lake and that. You wouldn't want to spoil the effect of the new venture with some old-hat stuff alongside."

There was a further silence. Then, through the windy sighs and moanings of space—or could it conceivably have been time?—Samuel Stokes was heard to say something about a cascade, about a rustic bridge, about prospects and points of view. There was a note in his voice that was less harsh, even perhaps a little wistful.

"Marvellous!" said Grandpa. "Just the job! You've got a free hand, that's the point. Get the thing going from scratch."

The voice was becoming more and more indistinct.

There was mention of woodland rides and ornamental pools and a cupola in the classic style.

"Yes! Yes!" cried Grandpa enthusiastically.

The radio fizzled and faded. Tim turned the volume knob and a racing commentator came on, running out of breath at the last fence.

"I reckon he's signed off," said Grandpa.

They looked at each other. Tim switched off the radio. "D'you think it's going to work?"

Grandpa shrugged. "No telling, is there? But I should think there's a good chance."

"You were brilliant," said Jane.

Grandpa shrugged again, in modesty this time. "You think so? Well, one did one's best. He needs tactful handling, that chap. Now—how about getting stuck into some of this nosh-up?"

Some while later the children made their way back to Charstock. They were feeling pretty full, having eaten all the roast potatoes (the peanut butter stuffing had been a considerable success, if you liked that kind of thing) though not much of anything else. Grandpa had done his best by the other items, but there was still a lot left over, some of which went to the next-door neighbour's cat, which turned out to have an insatiable lust for stewed eel.

Tim splashed up the garden path and in at the front door, kicking his boots off on the top step first, with what had become an automatic and practised movement. There was a smell of macaroni cheese or something, not all that welcome just at the moment. His mother was saying things about the time, to which, when she saw him, were added more things about the state of his hands, hair and face.

At the table, he stared at the plate in front of him. "Actually, I'm not very hungry."

"And I know what that means," said Mrs Thornton crisply. "You've been at Grandpa's. What was it this time? Raspberry trifle and chocolate sauce? Meringues?"

"Stewed eel. And roast carp. And syllabub."

"Ha ha. And peacock pie, I suppose. Very funny."

"Actually," said Tim, "we didn't manage the peacock pie." He picked up his knife and fork and began to do what he could about the macaroni cheese.

The residents of Charstock went to bed that night, as every night for the last thirteen days, surrounded by water. They drew their curtains against the long quivering ribbons of reflection and turned off their lights to the sound of its gentle lapping. Some of them responded to its presence in their dreams, and had a busy night on seaside holidays, or crossing oceans in liners, or struggling single-handed with transatlantic yachts. Others, sleeping more lightly, woke once or twice to hear a faint rushing and gurgling, as though perhaps a wind had got up and were moving the waters about, creating currents where no currents had been; they turned over and went to sleep again.

Tim was the first to get up the next morning, which was in itself curious as he usually had to be dug out of bed by one or the other of his parents after everyone else was at breakfast. Later, he knew that he had felt, as soon as he woke, that something was not . . . not quite as usual . . . not normal.

Or what had passed for normal in Charstock for the last thirteen days.

He went through a cursory washing and dressing process and came downstairs, feeling hungry. The peanut-butter-stuffed potatoes were a long time ago now. He opened the kitchen cupboard, rummaged for cornflakes, plate and so forth, took the milk from the fridge, glanced out of the window to see what kind of a day it was and . . .

"Hey!" he shouted "Mum! Dad! Look!"

The lake had gone. There was the garden—and the Spenders' garden and the Harveys' garden—restored once more to a regulation state of green and brown. Admittedly, there was rather more brown than green since everything was covered with a nasty layer of mud, and there was a great deal of rubbish which seemed to indicate that Charstock had perhaps been none too choosy about what it threw into the surrounding waters. A couple of empty baked bean cans sat in the middle of the lawn, and on the Harveys' path was a muddle of detergent bottles and plastic bags. Mrs Spender was already out in her garden, scurrying to and fro collecting rubbish. "Oh!" they could hear her saying, "I could weep. I could just sit down and weep. My patio! My barbecue pit!" The temple, too, was looking oddly seedy, as though with the vanishing of the waters it had started to disintegrate.

"Well I'm blowed!" said Mr Thornton.

"It's as though someone pulled a plug out," said Mrs Thornton. "Just like that."

She couldn't, Tim thought, have put it better.

Charstock was already emerging, to explore and exclaim. Various theories were put forward; one lady would have it that it was all just a matter of the moon and the tides—there'd been this upheaval of some kind up there and now everything was all right again; someone else reckoned it might have been that pumping after all; others said darkly it was just a question of the authorities getting moving and had been all along.

Now it was a matter of clearing up. Council lorries came down that very morning, everyone lent a hand with moving the rubbish, mud was swept from paths and pavements. In the general bustle and excitement various things went more or less unnoticed, except by the people personally affected. The couple in whose garden the grotto had appeared, told by telephone that the floods had now receded, returned to find the grotto inexplicably reduced to a sad heap of rubble. Of the statues there was no sign; it was assumed that they had been stolen. "It'll have been those antique dealers from London," said the neighbour. "Come down in the night. Stop at nothing, people like that." The Spenders' temple went from looking seedy to positively dilapidated until it began to crumble at the base and eventually had to be knocked down and removed. Mr Spender thought the water must have got into the fabric; Mrs Spender promptly ordered a cedar frame greenhouse with louvre windows and low level staging from a different firm and stood over Mr Spender while he erected it, spelling out the instructions word for word and staring suspiciously at each plank.

The chairman of Great Maxton District Council came down and toured the estate, beaming as though the disappearance of the waters was his personal achievement. Mr Cramp of Stagg & Co. dared to show up; he was seen directing operations on the site of the unfinished houses, where the lorries and cement mixers were already moving in once more.

And in the fields alongside the estate the bulldozers were again active, chewing up the grass and gouging out enormous holes. Great Maxton Development Plan Stage Three was going ahead nicely.

It was indeed. Almost too well, perhaps. A day or so

later the rumours began to reach Charstock. They were having some sort of trouble at the park site: each time the surveyors taped out the area for the swimming-pool they'd come back next day and find it all different, as though someone had been tampering with it. They'd had to put in a night watchman, but he couldn't ever catch anyone, though he reckoned there were vandals coming up there with an eye to setting things on fire, such a smell of smoke as there was . . . And yet never anyone to be seen.

Then there was the way in which the very ground itself seemed to be against them. The foreman said he swore the place got up and shook itself when your back was turned—you could have a site levelled out and then when you came back to it, the damn thing would be sloping every which way. You'd have a trench dug and next time you looked at it the thing would have a ruddy great kink in it, or have started to go round in a circle. Some of the men, he said, were just about doing their nut.

There were these trees that turned up where they thought they'd cleared the ground of every stick the day before.

There were the foundation holes for the swimming-pool changing rooms that filled themselves in again, as regularly as they were dug.

There was the water.

It was the water that got Charstock interested. Several people went up to have a look, and came back to report, not without a certain malevolent satisfaction.

"Looks like it's the council's turn now," said Mr Harvey. "You never saw such a thing. They've a got a trench there filled itself up with water overnight and believe it or not it's got water-lilies growing in it. One of the blokes on the site swears he's seen goldfish. The foreman's roaring around wanting to know who's been playing funny tricks." He laughed.

Tim looked at Jane. "Let's go and see."

They collected Grandpa and made their way in a leisurely fashion along the track that led to the field in question. They could hear the chug of bulldozers and the slither of earth being moved around.

It was quite true about the trench. The water-lilies were a bit mangled, but trying hard, and there were some irises too; any goldfish must have been lurking in the mud at the bottom. Some harassed looking men were trying hard to pump the water out. "Ornamental canal," said Grandpa. "Yes, that's his style all right, our friend."

They wandered around. There was an atmosphere of unrest and agitation, over and above that natural to a place bustling with bulldozers, men and an assortment of machinery. A cluster of people stood staring down at the ground. Grandpa and the children approached. As they got near, they could see that water was again the problem. A small jet was gushing up from the grass.

"That," said Grandpa with interest, "is a fountain, if I'm not mistaken."

The foreman stared at the jet. He put his foot on it, as though to suppress it that way, and then withdrew it again hastily. "Quite a bit of pressure there. Extraordinary. I never saw anything like it. A spring of some kind, that'll be."

"Fountain," said Grandpa. "If I were you I'd build a nice basin with some sculpture and make a feature of it."

The men looked round in annoyance. "Yes," said the foreman. "I daresay. Point is, this is the middle of the football pitch. And no visitors to the site, if you don't mind, sir," he added.

"Right you are," said Grandpa amiably. "Didn't mean to intrude. I can see you've got your problems." As they walked away, he went on to the children, "Poor fellow, he's up against it, I reckon."

They headed back to Charstock. It was evening and the sun was getting low in the sky, flaming the windows of the houses with pink and gold, but there was no longer that eerie surrounding glitter of the lake. Cars were homing after the day's work; washing hung out; children whizzed around on bikes. The gardens, tidied up and drying out, were green and leafy; indeed it was these, with their squares of lawn and their newly planted trees, that seemed to tether the place down, give it a settled look, as though it had arrived and were here to stay.

For hundreds of years. Or not, as the case might be. Tim thought again of successions of places, all on the same bit of ground; forests, maybe, and then fields, and then houses, and then something grand and a bit mad like Samuel Stokes's park, and then more houses and gardens. . . .

He said, "It's just as well everyone wasn't like him. Old Samuel thing. Being able to do what he can."

Grandpa stopped. They had reached the point where he turned off for his cottage. "It's very unusual, I'd say. Combination of circumstance and personality. Very interesting. Not the sort of thing these scientific johnnies will ever be able to get to grips with, though, in my opinion."

"Do you think it's ever happened before?" said Jane.

Grandpa considered. "There's no knowing, is there? Mind, it could have done, and you'd get people missing the point because of insisting on thinking in straight lines Very inflexible, people. Whereas . . ."

"Whereas we cottoned on?"

"Exactly," said Grandpa. "Bit of imagination, that was all that was needed. All's well that ends well. I'll be off home now."

That ends well . . . But of course it has not ended; indeed it looks set to go on for a long time yet. Sometimes Great Maxton District Council seems to be winning, and at other times it is clear that Samuel Stokes has got the upper hand. The football ground is laid out now and indeed Great Maxton and District have played their first match (a nil-nil draw) against Wittlebury and Pawton. But for some reason, whatever the weather, the centre of the ground is always sopping wet, at times the water fairly jumps out. And the cricket pitch has this upheaval at one end that no amount of rolling and mowing can get rid of, as though it were determined to turn itself into a hill. As for the cricket pavilion, it's a laughing-stock: people say it looks more like a classical folly than a cricket pavilion. The architect was just about in tears over it at first: he said that wasn't what he had in mind at all, and he can't for the life of him understand what went wrong. Five Chairmen of Great Maxton Council have resigned in succession.

Charstock, of course, watches with amusement. Sometimes people go up to offer advice, such as Mr Harvey when all those box hedges kept growing up through the new tulip-beds in the formal gardens. The children's playground has had the council workmen properly foxed: fast as they laid out the sandpit and paddling pools they'd find them filling up with peculiar plants or sprouting decorations of shells and fantastic carving.

You may well have read about it in the papers. The Maxton Affair, they call it, and usually it's pretty jokey stuff, as though folk down in those parts were a bit dotty and just playing the whole thing up. But some people have taken it seriously: a question has been asked in Parliament, and the professor from that university is still sending out his teams of investigators. His book is going to be published next year, for all the good that that will do. There has been another ministerial visitation; more men in dark suits have gravely toured the site, asking questions and taking notes. This time, nobody jeered or threw things, but the fumes of tobacco smoke were such that the visitors kept looking about them in perplexity.

All sorts of explanations have been put forward, from chemical contamination of the soil to sinister interference by a foreign power to the action of sunspots. A little old lady in Bristol who is a dab hand with the crystal ball and correctly predicts the outcome of the Cup Final and the Grand National every year, says it is due to the reawakening of the magician Merlin. A gentleman in Stoke Poges who deals in weather forecasting puts it down to volcanic activity.

We know better. Samuel Stokes has been diverted; whether he will ever be well and truly laid to rest is another matter. As Grandpa says, it's a question of personality and temperament, and feelings, and such things haven't got much time for the scientific approach.